MY COUSIN, THE ARAB

My Cousin, the Arab

BY THELMA NURENBERG

ABELARD-SCHUMAN
LONDON NEW YORK TORONTO

To Charles

LONDON	NEW YORK	TORONTO
Abelard-Schuman	Abelard-Schuman	Abelard-Schuman
Limited	Limited	Canada Limited
8 King St., WC2	6 West 57th St.	896 Queen St. W.

Printed in the United States of America

Foreword

Since their exile from Palestine in 135 A.D., when they revolted against the Romans for national independence, the Jews continued to pray for the restoration of their homeland to which they might one day return. This story is about a group of vibrant young people who, with others like them, laid the groundwork for rebuilding that homeland. It is about the dangers they faced — the challenges — and the rewards, as they struggled together facing what seemed like insurmountable obstacles.

To understand the background of this vital and moving story, some knowledge of the past is needed. In 1870, a group of Russian-Jewish students organized a movement called "The Lovers of Zion" and established farming communities in Palestine. The movement gained ground when, in 1897, Dr. Theodor Herzl founded the Zionist Organization, which proclaimed the right of the Jewish people to a national revival in their historic homeland.

This right was acknowledged by Great Britain when it issued the Balfour Declaration in 1917, and it was endorsed by the United States and the League of Nations.

Great Britain was given a Mandate at that time to rule over Palestine. Arab leaders whose countries had been liberated from Turkish rule by the British Army approved the Declaration, and Emir Feisal (later King of Iraq) signed an agreement with Dr. Chaim Weizmann, president of the Zionist Organization, saying that all necessary measures would be taken to encourage the immigration of Jews into Palestine as quickly as possible.

In a letter to Professor Felix Frankfurter, who later became a Justice of the U. S. Supreme Court, the Emir wrote: "We Arabs, especially the educated among us, look with the deepest sympathy on the Zionist movement. *We wish the Jews a most hearty welcome home.*"

The Zionists bought land in Palestine (Arabs were protected from displacement by the Transfer of Land Ordinances) and the work of reclaiming an underpopulated wasteland began. The young workers drained malarial swamps, cleared stony deserts, built modern health facilities, hospitals and schools and lived in peace with nearby Arabs who also benefitted by these improvements.

With Hitler's rise to power and the outbreak of war, getting into Palestine meant the difference between life and death for countless Jews, and attempts to immigrate there intensified. But the British government, hoping to neutralize Arab leaders, issued a "White Paper" in 1939 which drastically reduced the number of immigrants allowed to enter Palestine. Immigration was then suspended entirely for six months. The White Paper failed to achieve neutralization, however, and Arab leaders stepped up their activities against the Jews in Palestine.

Survivors of concentration camps, whose families and homes had been destroyed, now risked their lives to reach Palestine. But most of them again found themselves behind barbed wire. Not until 1947, when the

General Assembly of the United Nations agreed on partition and adopted a resolution for the establishment of a Jewish State in Palestine, was Israel —after nineteen hundred years — able to resume its existence as a sovereign state.

GLOSSARY OF FOREIGN WORDS

abayah (Arab.) cloak
batlan (Heb.) idler
chaverim (Heb.) comrades
dunum (Heb.) ¼ acre
echud (Heb.) Arab-Jewish unity
effendi (Arab.) (title of respect)
El Mahleh Rahamim (Heb.) Mourners' Prayer
Ernchen (Ger.) (affectionate term for Ernst)
Fawzi el din Kawkji (Arab.) Syrian leader of invaders
fellaheen (Arab.) peasants
gemütlich (Ger.) cozy
gemütlichkeit (Ger.) coziness
gibborim (Heb.) heroes
Haganah (Heb.) Israeli army
hamdu'illa (Arab.) praise be to Allah ("Thank God")
heimweh (Ger.) homesick
hora (Heb.) round dance
itbah lel Yahud (Arab.) kill the Jew
Ivrith (Heb.) Hebrew language
kalyinoot (Heb.) anemone
kefiyah (Arab.) Arab headgear
khamsin (Arab./Heb.) Eastern desert wind
kibbutz (Heb.) collective agricultural settlement
kibbutzim (Heb.) (plural of above)
kumsitz (Heb.) tea party
ma'asha (Arab.) communal land
maharba (Arab.) Welcome! Welcome twice!

mufti (Arab.) Arab religious leader
mukhtar (Arab.) head of Arab village (mayor)
mutti (Ger.) mother
naturlich (Ger.) naturally
nu (Heb.) (an expression) "so?" "well?"
palmach (Heb.) commandos of Haganah
rebabi (Arab.) one-string musical instrument
sabba (Heb.) grandfather
sabra (Heb.) (native Israeli)
Salaam Eleichum (Arab.) Peace be unto you
sanga (Arab./Heb.) cave; large boulder
Schechina (Heb.) Divine Presence
Shabbat (Heb.) Sabbath
Shabbat shalom (Heb.) Peace to the Sabbath
shaitan (Arab.) devil
shalom (Heb.) peace
Shalom! Hacol beseder. (Heb.) Peace! Everything okay.
shalom uvracha (Heb.) peace and blessing
shelanu (Heb.) ours
shema (Heb.) to hear
shuk (Arab.) store
succoth (Heb.) booth or hut for Succoth Holiday (usually trimmed with branches and harvest plantings)
Succoth (Heb.) Succoth Holiday
tante (Ger.) aunt
todah (Heb.) thank you
vattik (Heb.) veteran
wadi (Arab.) dry river bed
walla! (Arab.) (exclamation) "Good Lord!"
yekki (Ger.) German-Jewish refugee
yihye tov (Heb.) all is well
zemiroth (Heb.) table hymns

PART ONE

Chapter One

It was not until she saw the Egged bus to Galilee that Emmi felt the full crushing impact of her homesickness. There was something frightening in the mere act of climbing the bus, something final — as if she could never go home again. Her ticket was stamped July 8, 1947, and she was two days late. Would the driver accept it?

Lifting her brother Erni into the bus, Emmi settled him in the aisle seat as Avram had cautioned her. She felt uneasy at Erni's docility. In the three weeks of his illness he had become bony thin. His face seemed to have shrunk and his nose had grown longer. He looked so unhappy that she longed to console him with a lie — that soon they would be homeward bound.

On the other side of the bus, the three windows shattered by Arab sniping had been replaced by wooden slats. Slivers of glass lay imbedded in the cracks of the floor, and the air was faintly sulphurous with gunsmoke.

Opposite Emmi sat an old bearded man bent over a book. Earlocks dangled from under his flat round hat. His Semitic face was very much like the one her school paper had featured the day they had found out about her father.

"Don't hold on to your memories — the good or the bad," Tante Emmi had said. "They'll only trap you in the past.

And don't make comparisons. Germany and Palestine are not only two different continents. They are different worlds..."

Dejectedly, Emmi put her arms around Erni.

He shook her off, hating her now. Always, before, he had only to ask for something and Emmi would fetch it; he had only to wish for something and she would promise. And Emmi always kept her promise. Always!

But now, she had not only refused to do what he asked, but refused even to *promise!* Why was it so impossible? All they had to do was go back home exactly the way they had come. Even on the same ship! He had seen it at the pier only yesterday. He would have gotten on it if the Britishers hadn't been standing there with rifles.

He was sick of this wretched country with its filthy crowds and foul smells. Everyone was so un-German looking! And all this gobble-gobble of foreign talk. He wanted to be back in his beautiful Erlangen. Even the sections that had been bombed looked better than Haifa. He wanted to be in his own home, in his own room. And he wanted to walk down Koenigstrasse with his dog, Bubi.

If they did not return home soon, he would be late for school. Of course, he did not believe Emmi when she said they were going to live here forever. As soon as Mutti came, she would agree with him that this was a filthy country, and she would take them home. Mutti always did what he asked her to.

"Emmi, the bus stinks. Let's go to the Jew's truck," he said.

Flushing, Emmi gave a sidelong glance to see if the others had heard. She whispered, "You did not like it with Avram on the truck. Besides, it is filled with stuff he has to deliver."

"Emmi, I will vomit if we don't get off at once!"

"Ernschen, please! What will Mutti say when she comes and I tell her how naughty you were, running away yesterday . . ."

"I want to go home!"

"Ernst! Stop it at once! Mutti is waiting in Italy for the visa, and then she will come and we will all be together again!"

"I will vomit!"

She pinched his arm hard. "You will not! A German boy does not disgrace himself in public!"

Erni must be threatening to run away again, Paul Heller thought as he climbed into the bus. Emmi smiled wanly at him. He pitied her — for a kid of seventeen, she certainly had a tough responsibility thrust on her. And she was assuming it capably. But Erni, with his sense of German superiority, was creating more problems for her than she could cope with. Paul was rather sorry for the boy, though. All he wanted was to go back home — not an unreasonable demand for a youngster that age.

Emmi and her brother had been staying in the same hotel in Haifa as Paul, and from Avram, Paul had learned that they were to live in Kibbutz Tel Hashava, the same *kibbutz* that he himself was to live and study in for a year —on a Harvard Fellowship. Their Aunt Emmi, the *kibbutz* doctor, had met them on their arrival, found Erni sick, and had him hospitalized. While Emmi waited in Haifa for his recovery, their aunt had returned to the *kibbutz*, where she was killed during an Arab attack.

When Paul first saw Emmi in the hotel lobby, he thought her very pretty, although rather lifeless. She was wearing her pale blond hair in a braided coronet and her delicate face, with its small arched nose, had a moody look. When Avram introduced them, therefore, Paul was not prepared for the reflective depths of her eyes or the haunting quality of her slow, hesitant smile.

Emmi seemed too passive for one so young; Paul attributed this to a self-control that she must have developed through a burden of troubles, or some crushing frustration. He thought it was the latter when, after she had attended a concert with him and several music students, she revealed a depth of musical knowledge that was amazing for a girl of seventeen. She dismissed his question — had she prepared for a concert career? — with a shrug.

It was a pity that her mother had not arranged for them to live in America, Paul thought. He wondered how such a sensitive girl would adjust to the hardships and dangers of life in a primitive frontier settlement. Well, he had a full year to find out. But already he felt pessimistic.

Emmi quickened when Constable Alan Duffy climbed into the bus. He was in uniform now, and she thought that he looked quite dashing. Would he remember her? Greet her? It was only yesterday that he and Paul had gone looking for Erni, but Emmi felt that she wasn't pretty enough for him to have remembered her.

And, she admitted guiltily to herself, she only liked Alan Duffy because he resembled Gunther. He had the same narrow, long-jawed face and brown hair that sprang from a steep forehead — and the same bright blue eyes. Of course, the Britisher was older; Gunther was only nineteen. And Gunther must be forgotten now, even though he no longer wore the brown uniform with the swastika arm band.

Alan smiled at her and Emmi felt good noticing his warm friendliness. Roughing Erni's hair, Alan said with a mock gruffness, "Now don't you run off again! Next time, it will be an unfriendly *Arab* who will find you — and that won't be so jolly for you!" Erni giggled.

It was stifling in the bus. Sweat streamed down Erni's face and Emmi reached into her purse for a handkerchief. The flap of Tante Emmi's letter was stuck to the handkerchief and gently, she detached it. One of Tante Emmi's letters had robbed Emmi of her father, she remembered, and this one had robbed her of her homeland.

Emmi was fifteen when the letter came and it had set her thinking about problems that were not those of a child. These problems gnawed at her even when she was at the piano — those five hours of each day that should have banished everything sad from her mind.

The letter urged them to come to Palestine. Emmi's mother had been overjoyed at receiving it, since she had believed Tante Emmi dead. But Emmi had felt shattered. If they left Germany, she would never see her music master again, and Herr Professor Mahler meant more to her (excepting Mutti, of course) than anyone. And besides — never to see Gunther again! Really — it was impossible!

Suddenly not to be a German — but a Jew — and to live only with Jews! It would be like — like suddenly being somebody else, and not your own familiar self! Emmi knew she ought not to feel this way about going to Palestine. Mutti didn't, and Mutti was pure Aryan — the daughter of Pastor Dortweiler!

Even before the visas came, Mutti went about planning for the move to Palestine. She even tried to find tutors to teach Emmi and Erni Hebrew. But none of those who returned to Erlangen from the concentration camps knew the language.

It was childish to long for what could never be, Emmi

told herself. She must put Gunther and Erlangen completely out of her mind. And she must accommodate herself to
the life here and appreciate all the wonderful things that
were being done. Mutti had said this, before they had parted in Italy.

The bus began climbing. The confusion of domes,
massed roofs and white walls which Emmi had seen from
below now sorted into mosques, churches and balconied
houses surrounded by gardens. Below, along the shore, the
towers of oil refineries thrust upward above long, barrack-
like buildings.

Haifa Bay curved inland, to lap against the dunes of the
crescent-shaped land. A grim British man-of-war and a few
large passenger ships were anchored in the bay. Against
them, the dhows lifting on waves looked like driftwood.

Farther out, Emmi could see a rusty tramp steamer, its
black hull riding at anchor. Three British patrol boats,
their guns fixed, formed a barricade around it. The night
before, Emmi had heard that this was the ship carrying illegal immigrants who had been caught at sea. She had frozen with fear and panic, but Paul and Avram had assured
her that this ship had sailed from Hamburg, while her
mother's would be sailing from Italy.

To the right of the road the land rose gently, enfolded by
the Carmel hills. Its slopes were tufted with firs and silvery
olive trees. The fields were already brown, interspersed
here and there with vivid poppies and bright daisies. A
row of flat-topped concrete houses stood on the brow of the
hill.

What would the houses in Tel Hashava be like, Emmi
wondered. Tante Emmi, in her letter, had written, "One
cannot compare a new *kibbutz* with anything in one's expe-

rience. It is quite a primitive settlement, in which the most advanced social ideals are practiced. Everyone works hard — there are no luxuries. Often, the food is poor, but there are compensations in more basic values, and in comradeship . . ."

If all this seemed too abstract for Emmi to visualize and understand, one thing was abundantly clear — she must give up all thought of a concert career. And she must forget Herr Professor Mahler's parting words to her, for she could not practice five hours a day when there was no piano!

Thinking about all this, Emmi felt suddenly bitter with resentment. She had lost too much — her father, her school, her beautiful home, her Tante Emmi — and now, the career that she had been destined for. Then, because at seventen she had already learned that the miserable have no alternative but hope, she consoled herself with the thought that when Mutti came, she would make arrangements for a piano. Mutti was wonderfully clever and resourceful, she knew.

Yes, all that was best in their former life would be restored, once Mutti came.

Erni was asleep. A smile twitched at his mouth and he made a clucking sound that brought Bubi loping over to him. Emmi wondered how long it would be before a scab would begin forming over that part of his mind that held the past — and held it so tenaciously that everything *here* was fiercely rejected. Poor little Erni — who wanted nothing changed unless he changed it himself!

What would it be like for him in Tel Hashava, where every child was treated alike and equality began in the crib? How would they meet the special needs of this sensitive boy, accustomed since birth to being the pet of his family?

And how would Erni react to living with a group where sharing was a basic principle — he who had always been fiercely possessive?

The country of Erni's birth had been the cleanest and the best in the whole wide world, he thought. It was his longing to return that had made him run away yesterday. Emmi felt that she would never cease being grateful to Alan Duffy and Paul for finding him.

Snatches of their conversation reached her. Paul must have said something amusing, for they broke into laughter. Emmi smiled. It was good to share laughter; those who shared laughter agreed on something, and this was good! Emmi wondered if she would ever see Alan again after they left the bus.

It was a pity that Emmi and her brother were to live in Tel Hashava, Alan thought. The little nipper was tough-skinned and selfish, but Emmi was different. She was very shy and gentle and, remembering how savagely the raiders had attacked the *kibbutz,* Alan pitied the girl for having to live there.

She was very sweet; he hadn't seen anyone like her since he left England. He wished she weren't going to the frontier settlement; with the United Nations Committee proposing partition, things were shaping up to real trouble.

But Alan was glad that Emmi would be living so close to his post. How else would he be able to see this slip of a girl who smiled that sweet, gentle smile that made him want to put his arms around her protectively. Of course, he'd have to be clever to get to the *kibbutz;* the captain didn't want his men getting friendly with the settlers. It might give the Arabs the idea that they were taking sides with the settlers. But he'd find a way.

A white concrete building loomed in the distance. From a roof pole, a flag hung limply. As the bus sped closer, Paul saw that it was a Union Jack and that sandbags hugged the building. A line of pickup trucks and military vehicles stood behind a stone wall which was set off from the road by a barbed-wire fence.

The bus drew up to within a few feet of the post. Picking up his valise, Alan nodded unsmilingly to Paul and hopped down. Paul felt nettled; it was as if, with this abrupt and impersonal nod — within sight of the police post — Duffy had disclaimed knowing him, and that in any future encounter, they were to ignore each other.

Up ahead, Avram waved from his truck.

"We get off here," Paul said to Emmi. She woke Erni up.

"Where is Constable Duffy?" Erni asked.

"He left. He did not say good-bye because — because you were asleep," Emmi explained. But she felt dejected as she spoke. The Britisher had not thought enough of her to say good-bye. Yes, she thought, he was very like Gunther, an altogether different person in uniform.

Avram stood waiting for them at his truck. An Arab in a shiny red car honked for him to move over. Emmi saw Avram motion him on — the road was wide enough for both vehicles. The Arab honked again, then shouted angrily. Avram ignored him, folded his arms, and propped himself against the side of the truck. The Arab careened past him, spraying a cloud of dust and pebbles into the air as he went.

"Avram could have moved his truck," Emmi said to Paul.

"That Arab could have made it with his eyes shut," Paul replied. "In this country, you stand your ground or get knocked down."

Just the same, Emmi thought that Avram was too cocky. And homely! — With fuzzy black hair that made him look wild. His face, with its flat-tipped nose, had a hard, rugged look as if it was carved out of rock. And his sharp black eyes were either taking your measure or putting a question mark after anything you said. Or else they seemed to be laughing at you.

Avram smiled when Emmi reached the truck. He looked much nicer when he smiled, she thought. His strong, even teeth flashed white against his bronzed skin. He swung Erni onto the truck and then waited, his hands on his hips, for Emmi to climb on. He had no manners, Emmi thought, when he did not offer to help her. He was really a boor.

Avram was only nineteen years old, but Emmi could not compare him with any youth she had known back home. Alan Duffy and Paul kept reminding her of this one or that one, but Avram was entirely different from anyone she knew. Perhaps he was a type that represented the native-born Jew in Palestine, she thought.

The truck was crowded with farm implements and sacks of provisions. And in the rear stood an old, upright piano!

"Oh!" Emmi cried out, staring in disbelief.

"Junk!" Erni hooted, dismissing it with a wave of his hand. "At home, we had a grand piano and Emmi gave concerts and . . . ouch!"

She had pinched his arm.

"Good for us! She can give concerts here," Avram said.

They left the coastal highway, turning east. In the distance, Gilboa rose to steep, barren peaks, with huge boulders jutting out of its folds. The curse that King David had called down on Gilboa held it desolate, as a grim reminder throughout time.

They passed a huddle of mud huts that blended drably into the bare hills. Avram veered the truck sharply to avoid hitting a woman who was stooped over on the road. Wrapped from head to foot in a dusty, black gown, she looked like an oversized crow as she gathered dung with her bare hands.

The road ran parallel to a low range of hills whose bareness was broken here and there by a clump of low, gnarled trees. It is really quite ugly, Emmi thought.

"I want to go back to Haifa," Erni cried.

"We can't!" Emmi whispered. "Be quiet!"

"I will run away! I will!"

"Run away, then! You will never see Mutti again, if you do!" Erni glared sharply at his sister and then began sobbing into his fists.

The truck turned along a narrow dirt road now, beside which ran a wire fence. Beyond it rose some box-shaped buildings and then a row of tents. Giraffe-like, a watchtower thrust its long wooden neck above them.

"Tel Hashava!" Avram announced cheerily.

Chapter Two

Emmi stood up to look into the *kibbutz* and her face went blank with shock. Tel Hashava had a raw, bleak, unfinished look. Between two rows of tents, she could see a few small wooden huts and a long, concrete, barrack-like building fronted by a wide lawn. Marigold bushes brightened the seared, dusty look of the grass. In the distance, she saw a stand of young trees, so small that they looked like shadows on the ground. Beyond, the scrubby land climbed steeply to a rock-strewn hill.

The truck drew up before the concrete building and a man's voice called out, "Did you bring them?" Then Emmi heard the crunching of footsteps and a white-haired man appeared whose ruddy face beamed with welcome.

"*Shalom,* my children! I am Noah! *Shalom!*" he cried, swinging Erni to the ground. Then, turning to Emmi, he exclaimed, "You look exactly like your Tante Emmi!"

Emmi smiled, thinking this must be Noah, the *vattik,* the founder of Tel Hashava. Noah put his arm around Emmi's shoulder and took Erni's hand. He began walking them to the building.

"Well, young man! It hasn't been very pleasant for you, going straight away to a hospital! But we'll soon put some flesh on your bones and a tan on your cheeks! Yes, you will like it here! And for a special welcome, we have a newborn calf and a kid! The children celebrated by not going to school. Quite naughty of them, but then we do not have a calf and a kid born every day!"

As Noah chattered away, his hand pressed Emmi's shoulder. It was a wordless message that they were already friends and she felt it like an enfoldment. She looked anxiously at Erni, pleading silently for him to like and accept this dear old man.

Warily, the boy looked up at Noah. With his plume of white hair, twinkling blue eyes and round, ruddy face and nose, he looked very much like jolly old St. Nicholas. And he spoke an English that was almost as good as his own! "What's your name?" Erni asked.

"Noah. But you call me Sabba. In Hebrew, that means grandfather."

"Sabba!" Erni chuckled.

"Good! Already, you speak Hebrew!"

Emmi smiled with relief.

Two carts filled with young men and women came clattering up the road. Suddenly, children appeared and ran toward them shouting. A slender, black-haired girl in a khaki blouse and dark shorts jumped down from the first cart.

"That is Ora, my granddaughter." Noah told Emmi. "You are to share her tent."

The girl walked over to them in a swift, evenly paced stride. *"Shalom, Emmi!"* she said, offering her hand.

Emmi felt as if fingers of steel had clamped hers. She smiled shyly, awed by the girl's dark beauty and self-assurance. But Ora's look of cool appraisal disconcerted her. She seemed too haughty and self-important.

Ora greeted Erni as if he were an adult. Instinctively, he felt that he had shaken the hand of authority. Bobbing his head in a jerky bow, he edged closer to his sister.

"Sabba, I will see them settled," Ora said to Noah.

"Good! I must welcome the American student. Emmi, you see me later, when you are settled. We will talk then, yes?" Patting Erni's cheek, Noah hurried away to find Paul.

Ora led Emmi and Erni to the children's section, at the far end of the long concrete building. Just as they reached the door, two little boys ran out. Ora called after them and they came back reluctantly, with an impatient rush of words.

"Erni, this is Yaacov and this is Yigal, your roommates. They said they have already eaten and must hurry to tend the newborn animals, but they welcome you."

The boys scampered away.

Ora led the newcomers into a room that contained four cots, a table and some chairs. The walls of the room were covered with vivid crayon drawings that were crude but decorative.

"That bed is yours," Ora said pointing to an unmade cot near a window. "Chaveh will make it up with linen, but after today, you must do it yourself. Now you will eat . . ."

"I don't want to eat," Erni said sullenly.

"But you haven't eaten all day!" Emmi exclaimed.

"I don't like it here! I want to go!"

"Where do you want to go?" Ora asked quietly.

"Home! To Erlangen, *naturlich!*"

Emmi put her arm around her brother but he shoved her away with a vicious jab of his elbow.

"Stop that at once!" Ora commanded. "You cannot go back to Germany, and you must understand this!"

"I can so!" Erni shouted defiantly.

"You *cannot,* because they don't *want* you there!"

"Oh, no!" Emmi caught her breath sharply.

"You are lying! I hate you!" Erni said, shaking his clenched fists at Ora.

·24

"Don't, Ernchen, everything will be all right," Emmi said consolingly.

"It will not be all right if you comfort him with lies," Ora said. "If he is old enough to be so patriotic about Germany, then he is old enough to know the truth!"

Emmi paled but she met Ora's eyes unflinchingly. "One should not speak that way to a frightened child. It is not right!"

Without a word, Ora strode from the room. Emmi uttered a strangled sob and dropped her face into her hands.

The unfamiliar sound of her weeping distressed Erni and he flung his arms around her. "Don't, Emmi, I'll be good. I'll do anything you want me to, only don't cry!"

Noah's hearty greeting made Paul feel truly welcome. As busy as the old *vattik* was, he had taken time out to inform himself of Paul's mission here and he expressed delight that Paul had chosen Tel Hashava for his doctoral studies.

As Noah and Paul walked toward the tents, Paul could hear someone chanting a psalm. Looking back, he saw a thin, Semitic-featured man whose dark, narrow face was fringed with a black beard. He was leading a mule toward a shed and tossed back his head as he walked, letting his rich voice soar out joyously.

"Psalm 147," Noah said. "That is Jehiel. He always begins and ends his workday with a psalm. He is the oldest of our Yemenites. There are more in our Haifa group." They approached the row of tents and Noah pointed briefly. "Here we are," he said.

A red-haired youth, whose face was covered with freckles, thrust his head through a tent opening.

"Shlomo, this is the American student..." Before Noah could finish his introduction, Shlomo seized Paul's hand

and cried; "Hello Yenk! I spik English! I you welcome!"
His eyes sparkled with achievement.

Noah leaped aside to head off a fleecy kid that was loping
wildly between the row of tents. Some children yelled at
him to stop. Paul could see Erni among them as they went
scrambling after the animal. He was glad that already, the
children were drawing Erni into their lives.

Later, that afternoon, Ora brought Emmi over to a tent.
It was surprisingly roomy, Emmi thought. The canvas
walls were taut and secured firmly to its wooden base. It
held two cots, a stool and a crudely made chest of drawers.
Tacked to the canvas was a Paul Klee print. There was no
mirror, but a picture of a boy and girl, in a silver frame,
stood on the chest.

"You can have the two lower drawers," Ora offered.

"I can keep my things in the trunk," Emmi said. Surely
when Mutti comes, she thought, and sees how primitive
this place is, we will not stay — especially now that Tante
Emmi is dead.

"May I?" she asked Ora, placing two framed pictures on
the chest. When Ora picked up the larger one, Emmi explained, "We took that when Tante Emmi left Germany.
Erni wasn't born yet."

"Your mother doesn't resemble her . . . they don't even
look related," Ora remarked.

"They weren't. Tante Emmi was my father's sister."

"Your friend?" Ora asked, picking up the second picture.

Emmi crimsoned. She should not have brought the picture, but at twelve Gunther was altogether different than
he was at nineteen.

Glancing at the youth beside Ora in the snapshot, Emmi
wondered if he was an Arab. Thick dark hair tumbled over

a high forehead, and a wild sweep of eyebrows met at the bridge of a bony, humped nose. He had a rather fierce, challenging look, Emmi thought. "Your friend?" she asked.

Ora's smile transformed her completely, making Emmi feel more at ease with her. A girl appeared then and said, "Ora, you are wanted."

"Emmi, when you are settled," Ora said, "go to the dining hall. Things will seem strange at first," she added, "but you will get to like it here."

"Oh, I am sure I will," Emmi agreed readily.

She had been wrong about Ora — had misjudged her. Ora hadn't left the boys' room out of anger; she had gone to tell the house-mother about feeding Erni and providing linen for his cot. And it was Ora who had brought the boys back, translating for them while they coaxed Erni to come with them to see the newborn animals.

Yes, it was going to be all right, Emmi felt. Everything here was crude, but Noah was so friendly — and Ora was not really a snob, after all. Mutti would come, and then everything would be all right!

But even before she reached the open door of the dining hall, Emmi felt nervous about going in alone. Those seated at the long tables seemed to blur into one big family as she peered in, and she felt herself an outsider.

She turned away.

"Emmi!" someone called.

Avram and the American, Paul, came hurrying after her.

"Aren't you well?" Avram asked.

"I am — it is just..." she stammered. They marched her into the dining hall and over to a table where Shlomo was shovelling food into his mouth. When Avram introduced him, Shlomo bobbed his head but kept chewing away with noisy relish.

"Shlomo has been practicing his English on Paul. Now it is your turn to suffer," Avram said, sitting down beside her.

Shlomo's apelike grin was so infectious that Emmi grinned, too.

"This year, Shlomo is going in for languages," Avram went on, still teasing. "Whichever class has the prettiest girls — that's the language our Shlomo selects."

"Is pleasure learn when girls be pretty!" Shlomo said.

"That makes sense," Paul remarked.

"If you wish, I will teach you German," Emmi offered.

"I wish — yes! English good — already I know!" Shlomo accepted.

Emmi glanced at the settlers at the other tables. They were in their early twenties and looked clean and suntanned in their white, open-necked shirts and dark shorts. Her eyes settled on a youth with a flower behind his ear. He had bushy blond hair and the broad, strong-boned face of a peasant, but his eyes were sensitive. Suddenly, as he said something to his companion, they twinkled roguishly. Emmi liked the sound of his voice — a resonant baritone.

The tables were long wooden boards on trestles and were cluttered with tin cans for cutlery, sugar bowls, jam pots and baskets of bread. Flies swarmed everywhere but the settlers did not seem to mind. It was really very messy and uninviting, Emmi thought, and she wished that Avram would not reach halfway across the table to pass things to her.

Ora came over and seated herself at their table. Avram introduced Paul to her and she nodded indifferently. "Oh yes, the American professor," she said.

"Thanks for upgrading me," Paul said.

With a tired sigh, Noah sat down next to Ora. He reached

for the salad bowl and she snatched it away from him, but not before he seized a scallion.

"You were told what to avoid!" she scolded.

Noah sighed resignedly. "In Palestine, our young have tongues — but no ears," he said in mock complaint to Paul.

"That's because too much nonsense is spoken," Ora said and with a light tug at Noah's hair, she got up and went to the kitchen.

Finished with their meal, the settlers began leaving.

"Come along, children," Noah beckoned. "I want you to meet our new *chaverim*."

They gathered around him as he began introducing them.

"...and this is Dov, from Hungary," Noah said pointing to the blond-haired youth with the flower behind his ear. An impudent grin stretched across the Hungarian's face as he shook hands first with Paul and then with Emmi. Emmi could see a concertina slung over his shoulder and she quickened with delight.

"Dov thinks nature is anti-Semitic," Noah went on. "Either it rains too soon or too late or too little or too much! He expects miracles in the Land."

"A miracle did happen, Noah. I found a sliver of meat in the stew," Dov said. He spoke in English as he sucked noisily at his teeth.

"And this is Dvora, our expert with poultry and animals." Noah patted the arm of a stocky girl with a round, pock-marked face, as he spoke.

"Avram brought books and newspapers, but no rooster," Dvora complained. "We need roosters..."

"You will have your rooster, I promise," Noah said. Then he introduced Paul.

"Another professor!" Dvora grumbled. "What are we — from another world or something — that they come to study us?" With a grunt of disgust, she stalked out of the room.

"She's our anti-intellectual," Dov said, grinning. "If it doesn't give eggs or milk, it's not worth her notice."

"Never mind, she's a hard, steady worker, not a *batlan* — a loafer — like you!" Noah wagged his finger at Dov.

Dov made a woeful grimace that started the girls laughing.

"Are these all the settlers?" Paul asked.

Noah shook his head. "Only half. The others are working in Haifa, and come back every Sabbath. They will come for good when we get our hill land. We expect this soon, our new land. Yes, we were a nation of farmers and herdsmen before the world put a pack on our shoulders and turned us into merchants. But the circle has come a full round. We're peasants again, in our own land!"

Why did they want to be peasants, Emmi wondered. Back home, peasants were looked down on — patronized, with a kind of affectionate contempt. She wished that Noah would stop his speechmaking. She felt too tired to listen any more.

Ora came in then with a tray of food. Glancing at it, Noah shook his head. "But this is for infants!"

Ignoring his protest, Ora set a plate of porridge and two eggs in front of him. "Now you eat! Every bit of it! And slowly!" she ordered.

"Eat in good health, Noah," said Bracha, the cook, a Goliath of a girl with a mass of short, dark curls. She was very homely, Emmi thought. Her short nose was almost flat and her large upper teeth protruded as if there was no room in her mouth for them. Everyone greeted her affectionately and as soon as she smiled and spoke, Emmi knew why. She radiated cheerfulness.

Bracha gripped Emmi's hands in hers. *"Shalom,* Emmi!" she said with a warmth that instantly melted Emmi's reserve. "You will like it here. Everyone is sister or brother to the other."

"That is how it is with us," Noah said. "But, don't judge us by your standards, Emmi, judge us by our *ideals* — and the way we try to work them into our way of life."

"Enough, Noah! Enough!" Dov waved his hands in protest. "Speeches are for the platform where you can't see us sleeping."

It was not dark yet, but already the hills were blurred by a thick, violet haze. Emmi remembered how lovely the houses on her street used to look when the lights sprang on, and how fragrant the earth and flower smells of the gardens were. Her eyes filled with tears.

"Heimweh?" Paul asked, smiling down at her.

"Yes, I am homesick."

"But how can you feel that way about Germany, after all that's happened there?"

Emmi was silent a long moment and then, with a quick lift of her head and almost defiantly, she said, "Only my mind knows this — my heart does not."

The question had gnawed at her with each pang of homesickness and she felt wrenched as from a guilty love. "My heart remembers the happy times — when I was a child. It remembers the home I grew up in, the street, the kind friends we had. One cannot hate one's friends because others were bad. How can I give up the *good* memories I have when they help me to forget the bad?"

"Try not to think back," Paul said gently. "You'll like it here — if you *let* yourself like it. They're a wonderful bunch of people." He took Emmi's arm and began walking with her.

"I am sure," she said tonelessly. "Do you think it would be all right if I looked in on Erni? It is his first night here, you know."

"Why not? I'll go with you."

Somewhere, Dov was playing his concertina and suddenly Emmi's spirits lifted. His tempo was too fast for the Brahms waltz he was playing and he finished with a few dramatic minor chords. Then he glided into an arpeggio, swift as lightning and as sharply clear. Suddenly, the air grew lively with a polka. He was really first rate! It felt good, listening to his playing, Emmi thought. Mutti would come, and all would be well she was sure.

Chapter Three

It was Ora's second dream about Hassan, her Arab friend, that week and it troubled her. She sat up shivering in the predawn chill and stared moodily into space. Hassan had taken possession of her dreams because during the day she forced him from her mind.

Lately, his letters were not as self-revealing as his earlier ones. They were longer but said less and left many questions unanswered. And the newspaper picture he had sent her was captioned: "Arab student on Rugby Team." Really! Hassan was becoming conceited!

Had he fallen in love with another girl?

She was roused from her thoughts by the guard waking those assigned to the new wheat field. She switched on her flashlight and a circle of light fell on Emmi. There was a sweet smile on her face, as one who had gone to sleep in contentment. Ora gazed at her and wondered what it was like to sleep untouched by a troubled love. Then gently, she woke her. "Had a good sleep?"

Nodding, Emmi slipped into the shorts and blouse she had gotten from the storehouse the night before. Ora pulled back the flap to air out the tent.

"Will I have time to see Erni before breakfast?" Emmi asked.

"A quick hello, and hurry back," Ora said agreeably.

Emmi could hear children's voices lifted in a screechy singing. But it was a chant rather than a song and sounded like teasing. Then a girl's voice broke in scoldingly and the singing stopped. As Emmi entered Erni's room, several small boys made snickering noises at someone crouching in a corner. It was Erni — and a girl was speaking consolingly to him.

Erni saw Emmi and ran to her with a strangled sob.

"The boys are in a teasing mood," said the girl, Rina, who was their teacher.

"But why are they teasing him?" Emmi asked.

The boys pointed to a wet mattress, and Erni fled.

"I know how difficult it is for him," Rina said. "Especially the first night — but he refused to eat breakfast and he says he will not go to school. Please persuade him."

"He hasn't done this since he was an infant," Emmi said. "I am so sorry," and she hurried after Erni.

The moment he saw her he ran behind the barn.

"Erni, don't run from me!" she pleaded and seized his arm. He wrenched himself free, but stood beside her with downcast eyes. Tears slid down his face.

"Don't feel ashamed, Ernchen. This happens when . . ."

"I hate them! They're mean! I want to leave . . ."

"But how can we? Mutti will come soon . . ."

"You will write her where we are."

"Please, Erni . . ."

"I will run away! You will see!"

She shook him roughly. "Stop it! You will go to school and behave! And no more nonsense about running away! Now go back and do exactly as Rina says! Go now!"

When Emmi spoke like this there was nothing else to do but to obey. He gave the stone at his feet a vicious kick and straggled back.

Ora wished that the American and Emmi had not been put on her team; they were new to the work and certainly would slow down the others. The virgin soil was hard as rock.

The plow clawed at the earth, turning it over in great chunks. Ora followed, picking up the clods of couch grass with her harrow and shaking them free of the parasitic weeds. The American and Emmi loosened the clumps with their rakes. To Ora's surprise, he was proving himself a good, steady worker.

She ought not to have been so unfriendly to him last night, but somehow Americans always provoked her to rudeness.

Americans were a very generous people, she knew. She had met American women who devoted themselves to the work of raising money for medical and child care in Israel. But she bitterly resented those who gave out of charity rather than from a reverence for the land and what was being achieved here.

No, it was not charity to reclaim a land from the dead waste of time and neglect, she believed, nor was it charity to build a national home for the survivors of the concentration camps. The Holy Land is to the people of Israel what the soul is to the body. This she believed passionately, and this was exactly what Americans failed to understand.

The land was like a flame inside her and she resented youths like Paul who came to observe — mere spectators — in this struggle for a national destiny.

She wished Paul had chosen another *kibbutz* for his study.

Several times that morning the plow struck rocks, but now one jutted out that seemed part of the earth itself — and as immovable. Shlomo was called from a nearby field. He came with Gittel, the mule, grinning broadly because Ora needed him.

They dug around and under the rock. Avram hooked an iron chain around it while Gittel pulled, but the chain kept slipping off. Paul covered the rock with a matting of dry weeds, and with a great neighing and baring of teeth Gittel strained forward. It was as if she were pulling the earth.

Suddenly, the rock budged and a shiny black snake, long and wrist-thick, slithered out. The mule brayed in terror, reared on its hind legs and bolted away. Emmi stood magnetized by the snake until it lifted its head. Then, with a cry, she ran blindly into Gittel's path.

"Emmi! Look out!" Avram shouted, as he tore after her, but it was Ora who seized her arm and snatched her to safety. The frightened mule galloped away, with Shlomo in pursuit.

Picking up the sobbing girl, Avram held her close, murmuring Hebrew endearments. When her panic subsided, his hands dropped from her shoulders and he turned away to examine the blades of the plow.

"Mice and snakes —" Emmi said apologetically, "they terrify me."

"This one was not harmful," Ora said.

"Just the same, it can give one an awful shock," Paul remarked.

Although some kind of shade from the burning rays that scorched the fields at noon was a necessity, it took a sensualist like Dov to make it a thing of near beauty. He had rigged one up on sticks using a square of canvas, trimmed with bright cotton streamers, for a roof. Emmi sat down under it with a sigh.

If Ora had not called a lunch halt, Emmi felt she would

have collapsed from sheer exhaustion. Every bone felt bruised and the flesh of her palms, for all the medicaments that Ora had applied, still felt raw. She was sweating all over and her face, she was certain, was dirt-streaked.

How long would they keep her doing such hard work? Already, her fingers felt as stiff as lead. They would lose their dexterity and be absolutely ruined for the piano.

If Alan Duffy came and saw her working like a common peasant, and looking like one, she would die of humiliation!

Her braids had become loosened and she began to plait them tighter. Dov caught at one as she began winding it around her head.

"Leave it loose for a bit," he said in German, curling the ends around his finger. "I like to see an old-fashioned girl with long hair."

That's an archaic luxury here," Ora said dryly, "and hairpins do not grow on trees."

"Long hair is nice to look at but foolish to wear, like an extra load on the head," Avram agreed. "But I can always find some wire to make you hairpins," he added quickly when he saw the hurt look on Emmi's face.

Mischief twinkled in Dov's eyes. He took the flower from the visor of his cap and tucked it into Emmi's hair, saying to the others in Hebrew, "Agreed then, the majority votes that Emmi's hair will not be a settlement problem."

"Not the majority," Ora said sarcastically. "The American hasn't expressed himself yet."

"The American thinks Emmi's hair is Emmi's business," Paul said dryly, and then, because Ora's hostility nettled him, he added, "Is it me or Americans in general you don't like?"

"I've nothing against Americans," Ora flung back. "They've been most *charitable*."

The significance of her last word did not escape him. "I know what you mean, but how else can we help?"

"Don't just give us money and think you've done your good deed. Soon we will be a State — the State of Israel — and here you will not feel yourself an alien."

"America is my native land," Paul said. "I don't feel myself an alien there. But I do, here."

Ora drew back as if Paul had struck her. Avram gave her a warning look. Ora was much too rude and dictatorial — she must not alienate Paul as she had the other Americans who had visited here.

Rising, she picked up her rake. The others stirred and work was resumed.

Weeding out the couch grass was finished late that noon. Then Ora signalled for everyone to return to the wagon.

The sun had burned an angry welt across Emmi's face. She wanted to cry from utter exhaustion but felt ashamed before the others. How had Erni fared? Had Rina been successful in coaxing him to school? Emmi sighed, thinking, surely if Mutti comes and sees how primitive it is...

There was room for the American in the wagon but he preferred to go on the tractor rather than ride with her, Ora felt. She had antagonized him, she knew, but then, he should not have flaunted his Americanism at her!

How ironic it is that Hassan, an Arab, felt himself in exile abroad while Paul regarded Palestine, the homeland of his ancestors, as an alien land! She sat with her arms looped round her knees, stabbed through with longing for Hassan.

Over the clatter of the tractor, Paul heard the Yemenite's flute-like chanting and he turned to look at him. There was something biblical about his appearance, the dark-hued, gaunt Semitic face fringed with beard; the dignified, even-paced walk of the man, as if deeply conscious of a belonging.

There must be a wonderful affinity between this man and God, Paul thought, to serenade Him at the beginning of the workday and at its close.

Avram turned in at the gate. Near it, a small boy squatted on his haunches. He glanced briefly at the two on the tractor and looked sullenly away.

"Erni must have made a nuisance of himself," Avram remarked. "He insists on remaining an alien. He has one thing in common with the Arab terrorists — they don't want us here, and he doesn't want to be here."

"It's tough on a kid to be where he doesn't want to be," Paul said.

"It's tougher yet to be where you're not wanted. It could even be fatal," Avram replied. "It was fatal for six million of us — only a few years ago."

Chapter Four

That Friday, Noah had company; his old Arab friend from the Jezreel Valley, Abu Sa'id El Khoury, and Sergeant Liam Cassidy. The latter came on official business, but that did not prevent Noah from enjoying his presence. The Britisher, although he looked like a disgruntled bulldog, was a good-hearted man and had proved himself a friend even though he always taxed the scant supply of the *kibbutz* whiskey.

Swallowing his drink in one quick gulp, Cassidy braced himself against the unpleasant task ahead — the *kibbutz* searchlight about which nearby Arabs had complained.

Abu Sa'id sipped at his third thimbleful of sweet black coffee. His dark face, with its bony, hooked nose and piercing black eyes, had the predatory look of a hawk. He wore a white *kefiyah* over his head and a white gown under his *abayah*, below which high, thick-soled shoes protruded, the only concession to western dress.

The three men were reminiscing, for they had not been together in several years. Abu Sa'id was, as Cassidy remembered when he had patrolled the Jezreel Valley, reserved in speech and manner, with a pessimistic outlook, while Noah was as talkative and optimistic as ever. The troubled years had neither subdued his spirit nor soured him on the Arabs.

Now why couldn't the rest of the devils — Jews and Arabs — live in friendship like these two, Cassidy wondered, instead of creating friction in the country?

Noah and Abu Sa'id were remembering an incident that had happened some fourteen years before, when Bedouins raided the Arab village in the Jezreel and Abu Sa'id had brought his grandchildren, Hassan and Ferial, to the Jewish *kibbutz* for medical treatment.

The two old friends were laughing now, over the mistake the foreign journalist had made in captioning pictures of Ora and Avram as the little Arab victims, and Hassan and Ferial as children of the Jewish pioneers.

"Now that Hassan is home from Oxford, what will he be doing?" Cassidy asked.

Abu Sa'id threw up his hands. "We old ones are no longer consulted. We are informed!"

"How are things in the valley?" Noah asked.

"Quiet. Jezreel is quiet," the Arab replied.

"Too quiet," Cassidy muttered. "And that means trouble."

"Only *Allah* knows what it means," Abu Sa'id remarked dryly. He rose.

"But you cannot leave without sharing our meal!" Noah protested. "Ora will be offended that you did not wait."

"I came only to ask you to the wedding of Ferial," Abu Sa'id said. They accompanied him outside and just as he was about to mount his horse, Ora came running toward him, her arms outstretched.

"Welcome! Oh welcome *Ya* Abu Sa'id!" she cried, embracing him.

Lightly, his fingers touched her cheek and then he kissed her forehead. "The daughter of your daughter is

41·

bright as a *kalyinoot* and even more beautiful," Abu Sa'id said to Noah.

Ora flushed. It was pleasing to be likened to the anemone, the first flower of spring. But Noah's rejoinder sent the smile from her face.

"I would the daughter of my daughter had her mother's wisdom, and not just her beauty."

"Wisdom is not lacking when the eye is so sharp," the Arab replied.

"Sabba is never pleased with me, *Ya* Abu Sa'id," Ora sighed. "But what news have you of Hassan?"

"You will not lack for news when you see him at the wedding." He mounted, smiling away Ora's protests that he eat with them, and rode off, straight-backed and proud.

"About the range of the searchlight," Cassidy said, turning to Noah. "The Arabs have complained. . . ."

"But we have already shortened the range! If we shorten it further, we'll be looking at our navels!" Noah protested.

"I'll have a look. Capt. Ainslee's orders," Cassidy said.

Bracha came running. She planted herself before Cassidy; with her hands on her hips, and eyed him critically. "Cassidy! You are getting too thin! Soon, there will be only bones in your uniform! Don't they feed you at the post?"

"You're the daft one, talking nonsense," he growled, as a few creases — a smile of sorts — appeared on his face.

Shaking her finger at him, she said: "You come in after the police business. I will make potato pancakes for you."

How many years had it been, Cassidy wondered, since he had found Bracha — then a young child — trotting along a road with a day-old kid clutched in her arms.

Behind her, lay the smoking ruins of a small *kibbutz*. He had brought her to Noah, in the Jezreel parent *kibbutz*.

Bracha became so attached to him that he found himself drawn to the *kibbutz* more often than his official duties required. He would come by on horseback and swoop her up in his arms as she came running over to him. Once, returning after two years' service on the northern border, he found her so grown that, in bending to lift her to his horse, he was pulled to the ground by her weight. He had called her Bracha, the Goliath, and since then the name had stuck.

But for all her tragic childhood, Bracha had a sunny disposition. Once — when she was six years old — Cassidy teasingly asked her to marry him. Later, he found her waiting beside his horse, with her belongings tied in a towel.

The grown Bracha had retained her sunny, good-natured disposition, although now and then, as when she teased him about joining the *kibbutz*, Cassidy had to be abrupt with her. Holy Mary, Mother of God! Himself baptized in the faith — and living in a Jew settlement!

Emmi flushed when Noah, in passing, gave her an affectionate pat on her cheek. The British officer looked grim.

"What does the officer want with Noah?" Erni asked.

"To see that things are in order," Emmi said, uncertain.

She was wearing her light-blue linen dress with the pink embroidery at the neck. Erni liked it when she wore her own pretty clothes rather than the unpressed blouse and shorts she wore all week. The settlers were dressed better, too — it was their Sabbath Eve. But no one looked as nice as his Emmi. Swaggering alongside her, Erni wished the children would look up from their playing to see what a beautiful sister he had. But Rina, his teacher, came toward them and he fled indoors.

"Shabbat shalom!" Rina greeted Emmi.

Self-consciously, Emmi returned the Sabbath greeting. She had attended Avram's Hebrew class every night that week, but the new words were an alien sound in her ears as she spoke them. "Is Erni behaving in school?" she asked.

"Too well," Rina smiled. "He answers neither me nor the children. He is the ghost in our class."

"He feels mortified ... the children tease ..."

"They don't any more," Rina said. "I explained it to them, and they try to be friends but he ignores them."

Emmi suddenly quickened with excitement as she saw Alan Duffy in the police pickup. She began fussing with a loose strand of hair. Would he remember her? Greet her?

".. and if you would only convince Erni that the children do want to be friends," Rina was saying. "He has been here one full school week already and he hasn't learned one Hebrew word!"

"He will do better — you will see!" Emmi promised. Her heart gave a wild leap now because Alan was looking at her.

".. and he can be happy here, if only he would let..." Rina left the sentence unfinished as Dov came down the road with a girl on his arm. Rina gazed after him with such yearning that Emmi felt a pang of sympathy for her. Dov, she knew, flirted with all the girls and was serious with none.

When Rina walked away, Emmi thought of going into the house and having a talk with Erni. But if she did, Alan might go off! She stood there, uncertain, when Erni ran out, shouting, "He is here! The constable — he is here!"

Seizing Emmi's hand, Erni began pulling her forward.

"Don't shout!" Emmi scolded, but allowed herself to be pulled along. She was glad that she was wearing a pretty dress. Alan came striding toward them. How like Gunther he looked!

"You've tanned!" Alan exclaimed. "You look fine!" Ruffling Erni's hair, he asked, "Well, my fine fellow, have we been good?"

"Yes sir!" Erni stiffened to attention.

Another constable was sitting behind the wheel of the pickup. With his brush-short yellow hair and his flat-tipped nose, Erni thought he looked German. Maybe he was German! Erni picked up a few pebbles and threw them aimlessly, edging closer to the pickup as he did so. But the constable sat as if Erni were invisible.

"Are you German?" Erni finally blurted out.

"Born here; German stock," the constable nodded.

"I am too!" Erni cried elatedly.

Looking down at the thin, Semitic face with its long nose and burning eyes, a smile twisted the constable's mouth. "So? Do you live here?"

"Only until Mutti comes. Then she will take us home."

"Don't you like it here?"

"I hate it! Mutti comes — and we go home!"

"Where is she now?"

"In Italy, waiting for the visa. That is my sister with Constable Duffy. Soon we go home!" he said gleefully.

"Does your sister say you will go home?"

"No, but that is her way of teasing. She says I must go to school and learn, so I can stay. But they won't send me away if I don't learn, will they? I must stay until Mutti comes."

"Then you had best behave yourself," the constable said over a yawn, and resumed reading his magazine.

Erni felt as if he had been dismissed.

Alan drew Emmi out of the path of two boys chasing each other. "Do you like it here?"

"It is not bad. Everyone has been most kind to me."

Emmi felt good about the relaxed holiday spirit in the air. Even the children sitting on the lawn with their parents had a scrubbed, festive look.

Four youths went past carrying something unwieldy, and Emmi's eyes widened. It was the piano! But her excitement subsided when they carried it into the dining hall. The room was a beehive of activity with nightly meetings; practicing there would be impossible.

"What have you been doing, Emmi?" Alan asked.

"I work in the fields. Today we planted wheat."

"Hard work, that. I should think they'd give you office work or something light."

"We rotate the work — all but the specialists. The first day was hard, though," she admitted. The palms of her hands were still blistered from those few days in the fields.

"What do you do in the evening?"

"I go to the Hebrew class. There are all sorts of meetings and committees and clubs. I may join their music club ..."

"Not much fun, meetings, I shouldn't think." He was silent a moment. Then, with a smile that was surprisingly shy, he said, "I'm due for a holiday in two weeks. Would you care to see a film with me in Haifa?"

"Oh yes, I would love it!" Emmi cried, crimsoning with delight. "But how could I get there?"

"I'd call for you, but — well — against orders . . ."

Just then, Cassidy came striding down the road, followed by Noah and Avram. With an abrupt "Must go, Emmi," Alan bolted away.

"Emmi, the other constable is German," Erni said, tugging at Emmi's dress. "His name is Karl!"

Emmi smiled distantly. Had Alan really asked her for a date?

The dinner gong sounded just as the police pickup sped out of the gate. Emmi brought her brother back to the children's section and he went in without his usual tantrum.

Avram's truck went rattling down the road. He honked the horn as he drove past Emmi, and called out something that she could not hear over the roar of the motor. She wondered what Avram would think if he knew about the date with Alan. Of course, it was not a definite date — but he did seem in earnest.

It was not until Emmi had gone past the children's section that she realized that *"Shabbat Shalom"* had been addressed to her. Turning, she saw Jehiel, the Yemenite — fresh from the shower — his dark curls glistening wetly under his skullcap. He was hurrying a small boy toward the wooden huts. She called back *"shalom uvracha!"* and Jehiel smiled and bowed. His dark, expressive eyes were very gentle.

Shalom uvracha! Peace and blessing. Avram had taught this last night at the beginners' class and she thought it was a lovely phrase. She repeated it softly to herself.

When she came into the dining hall she was struck by the change in its appearance. It smelled of soap and a fresh scrubbing. White tablecloths and field flowers in glass jars made the room look festive. Sabbath in a *kibbutz* was really quite jolly!

Soon, the room was crowded with unfamiliar faces. The Haifa members had arrived. Watching the affectionate reunion, Emmi suddenly felt herself an outsider. She looked around for Paul or Dov or Ora, but they had not come yet. She took the first vacant place at the table near Dvora, the anti-intellectual. Dov came then and Emmi felt relieved. He hooked an arm around her shoulder as he seated himself beside her and immediately jumped up again, staring at something in front with disbelief.

"Moshe our Rabbi! A piano! We're beginning to live!"

Pointing at it with her fork, Dvora spattered out, "No money for a rooster — but money for *that!*"

Dov considered her a moment and then grinned mischievously. "Tell you what, Dvora my love! I'll make a present of you to any *kibbutz,* together with my concertina and my right eye..."

A roar of laughter broke out but when Dvora looked hurt, Dov hugged her and said something apologetically. He was really very nice, Emmi thought, and jolly to be with, but he ought not to tease and flirt so much!

Hardly had the meal ended, when tables were pushed against the walls, benches placed in rows, and a meeting began. Reports that had been made during the week were to be discussed with the Haifa members, Dov told her.

She left the dining hall.

In the distance, Gilboa's peaks were flushed a pale rose under a sky that was spanned with streamers of orange, gold and pale green. Sunsets here made Emmi feel pensive. Slowly, the hues faded and a swirling mist, like a blue veil, began draping the mountain. Almost at once, Gilboa was a dark shadow massed against a cloudless sky.

Emmi heard a soft scrunching on the pebbled road and now Paul stood beside her. Neither spoke — absorbed in the beauty of oncoming night. The dwellings blurred into the dark. In one, candlelight flickered brightly against a window. Inside, Jehiel, his small son and his wife sat around a cloth-covered table. They were celebrating the Sabbath. The boy rocked as he sang in a thin, high-pitched voice. Naami, her dark, cameo face cowled with a white lacy scarf, had a sweet look of contentment. The golden spears from the candles in the handsome silver candlesticks shimmered against their faces.

A book lay open on the table and the three sang:

"Purify our hearts so that we may worship Thee truly."

"Oh, how happy they sound!" Emmi exclaimed.

Suddenly, the night quiet was broken by shouting.

"What is happening?" Emmi seized Paul's arm.

"Sounds like cheering," he said reassuringly.

They ran to the dining hall. The mad scraping of a violin and Dov's concertina could be heard over a jubilant singing and the rhythmic stomping of feet.

Arms linked, the settlers whirled around the room, kicking out the steps of the *hora*. In the middle, old Noah was stomping away crazily, his arms outflung, and plume of white hair tossing this way and that. Avram seemed to be bouncing on springs, while Dvora's eyes sparkled with happiness. Bracha swung past them, the zest of her dancing threatening the floor boards. Emmi marvelled at how happy and carefree they all were.

But the greatest transformation had come over Ora. She danced like a creature possessed, her eyes a flame of gypsy wildness. Paul watched her, entranced. Was this the shrew of a girl who had been needling him all week?

Avram reached out and seized Emmi.

"But I don't know the dance!" she protested.

"Step, stamp, kick!" and he hooked his arm tightly around her shoulder. Paul seized her other arm and closed the ring.

"What's up?" he shouted to Avram.

"The land! We've got the hill land!"

Emmi felt clumsily out of step.

"Hop to your right foot! You'll be in step." Avram pressed her right shoulder and suddenly the gay spirit caught her and all the resisting stiffness left her body.

"Good! You're with it now!" Paul said.

Step — stamp — kick!

The ring whirled faster now.She felt a marvellous lightness. Faces blurred; the walls whirled about her.

When it settled, she was back in Erlangen, dancing the round dance with Gunther.

They were returning from their holiday hike to the Harz Mountains — the pastor of the Frauenkirche and his wife and Helmut and Elsa and, of course, Gunther. They had reached the hills of home. Below, Erlangen looked toylike in a vast garden. Church spires glinted silver in the waning sun, but the turreted stone shelves that were the university walls came to her as a grim reminder that a holiday had ended.

And suddenly, they all linked arms and leaped into a round dance. It was an outbreak of ecstasy — the last gay moment of freedom before school chained them to an iron discipline. Gunther whispered in her ear. "We will go off by ourselves when we are older, when we marry."

She could hardly breathe with the joy of it. They were only twelve then, but Gunther had claimed her. The dreadful war would end and the years would pass as a moment! Gunther loved her, and she danced in ecstasy, knowing this.

Step — stamp — kick!

Seeing how Emmi abandoned herself to the dance, Paul felt good. She was dancing away her doubts and her fears and this, he felt certain, was the beginning of her oneness with Tel Hashava.

Chapter Five

Several days later, and unexpectedly, Emmi went to Haifa with Avram. He drove the battered old truck with remarkable skill, she thought, easing it smoothly around the sharp turns and slowing cautiously before the deep ruts in the road.

An hour before, when the Agency phoned about the registered letter in the Haifa post office, Noah himself had brought Emmi the news. He had been very concerned, and urged her not to be pessimistic. Her fright had been brief; she remembered that she had no living relatives in Germany. But if she told Noah this, he might decide that it was not urgent for her to go, and the prospect of a day in the city was too tempting for her to resist.

"Perhaps you will need money for the letter," Avram said. "I will give you . . ."

"Thank you, no. I have money," she replied.

"I will wait, so we can do the errands together."

Emmi's heart sank. The joy of a day to herself, of wandering leisurely through the streets, of visiting the lovely bazaars was not to be! Avram was spoiling it for her. "You are very kind, Avram, but it is not necessary for you to wait."

He glanced at her, puzzled. She was so very pretty that he could not bear her being cross with him, and for reasons he could not fathom.

"Since you wish it, I will not wait," he said edgily. "I will give you a list of places where you can meet me, and at what time. But don't be long. There is sniping. Haifa is a wicked city."

"Surely you are not serious!"

"I am very serious. The sniping you yourself saw on the buses. Also, there are assassins for hire and dope smugglers and worse! Girls like you are not safe there . . ."

"I lived there a month when Erni was in the hospital and I did not find it wicked. It is a most interesting city."

"Interesting, yes — but not safe for a girl alone. Noah will be very angry that I am leaving you alone."

"Then we need not tell him!" She said this with such finality that he frowned, suspicious. Had she a rendezvous — that she was so eager to be rid of him? Impossible!

The road twisted down the spine of the mountain and then looped around a ridge of hills that led to the coastal highway. Soon, they came to the lovely houses of Hadar haCarmel and Emmi wished that Avram would slow down so that she could enjoy the ride. Instead, he went plummeting down the hill road as if he had sensed her thoughts and relished being contrary.

Now the road plunged into the heart of the old city. Paved streets spanned out in every direction, and Avram drew up at the post office. He handed Emmi a batch of letters to mail and then wrote out a list for her.

"Don't lose this list!" and with an unsmiling nod, he drove off. Watching him weaving back into the stream of traffic, Emmi felt a sudden panic. She would meet him as soon as she picked up the letter. He would tease her about taking his warning seriously, but he would be pleased. She hurried into the post office with this resolve, and felt good about it.

When she saw the envelope with the stamp of the Bonn government, she stood with it unopened, feeling shivery with suspense. Perhaps it was from Gunther! She tore the envelope open. It contained a notice that, due to the nonpayment of taxes, the house on 54 Luise Strasse, Erlangen, had been foreclosed.

Emmi stared at it for a long moment, and then laughed.

"What's so funny? Or is it?"

It was Alan! She gaped, incredulous.

"But this is only Wednesday!" she cried.

"The schedule was changed. What made you laugh like that? It sounded, well, rather not funny."

"This," she said, and handed him the letter.

He was hatless, and wore a beige suit that accentuated the deep tan of his face. It was such a fine face, Emmi thought, so clean-lined and manly.

"The bloody swine . . . oh . . sorry!" He gave her back the letter.

"But it is not true!" Emmi cried. "Mother paid the taxes before we left. An old friend occupied it — he was trying to sell it for us. Mother will be very upset . . ."

"Well, no use worrying until she comes. You really wouldn't want to go back, anyway, would you?"

She shrugged, not trusting her voice. Would she! Where in all this world was home, but Erlangen!

"Lucky for me, finding you. Did you come with Avram? Must you rush back?"

"No, I need not." She felt giddy with joy.

"Good!" He took her arm. "I'll post this letter and we'll be off. Odd thing, I wrote my mother about you, in this letter. She wanted to know how you were getting along."

"About me?" Her voice went high with surprise.

"Yes. She likes to know everything about anyone I like."

Emmi flushed with delight.

Their lunch on the terrace of the Carmel Café was nearly over, and Emmi sat back and closed her eyes to enjoy the moment, to hold it inward so that she could recapture it against a later need. The handsomely groomed people dining in quiet leisure, the gleam of silver, the silky feel of a damask napkin in her hands — oh! — she had no idea how intensely she had missed all this!

What was she thinking of, Alan wondered, with that dreamy, faraway look? "Hello there, Emmi," he said softly.

Blushing, Emmi stammered. "I — I was wondering — if I shut my eyes and then opened them — would I really be here? It is so — so *gemütlich* — so very pleasant."

"Good! We'll do this again, shall we?"

Now the blood swept to her face; this was too wonderfully good to be happening to her. She nodded eagerly.

"How are things at the *kibbutz*? Do you like it?"

How could she tell him — a British constable — that she loathed it. That the day-to-day existence was very primitive — that she never knew a moment of privacy . . . .

"Oh, it is not too bad," she said. "Of course, it is altogether different from — from my life before. But things will improve . . . the *kibbutz* is quite new . . ."

"It must be dull for a city girl like you."

"Evenings, I take Hebrew lessons with Avram. They have a good choral group. Dov plays the concertina beautifully and Ora the flute. They are really very musical. It isn't dull. It's just — well — rather lonely."

"I know about loneliness, Emmi. Sometimes, it makes

me want to chuck everything and go home. It's such a terrible mess of a place — I shan't regret the day I leave."

A numbness went through her. "When will you leave?"

"Who knows? What with the Arabs on the rise, and those bloody Irgun terrorists. A nasty lot, I can tell you. The United Nations doesn't seem to be getting anywhere with this partition business. We're probably here to stay."

Emmi breathed out a long sigh of relief.

They walked the tree-shaded streets of Hadar haCarmel in a companionable silence that was broken only when they paused before a house that caught their fancy.

It seemed incredible to Emmi that this elegant suburb and primitive Tel Hashava were only thirty miles apart. This, she felt, was where she belonged. As soon as her mother came and saw it, she would make arrangements to live here. There was money enough, Emmi knew, and if the need arose she would find work, teaching music.

They came to the handsome Jewish Technical Institute, its lawns fringed with pines and lacy pepper trees.

"One thing about your people . . ." Alan began.

Emmi tensed.

" . . . wherever they go, they build schools right away . . ."

Some day she would have to determine what she was. Because her parents did not talk about it in front of the children, it had become a problem. — That day at school, for example, when her teacher had exposed her as a Jew and her classmates gaped at her as if she had sprouted horns before their very eyes. In her humiliation, she had not sought consolation or support in a national pride. In the years without school that followed, music had been her religion and her sustenance.

"You are quiet, Emmi. Are you tired?"

"Oh no! I — I was just thinking — something you said. I love to walk. Back home we went on long walks . . ."

"Good! We'll start on one now, shall we?"

Alan, Emmi found, was as familiar with the labyrinthine streets of the upper and lower city as if he had lived here all his life. He led her along narrow, twisting streets and cut through alleys until they reached Kingsway, the main street of the old Arab quarter.

They came into a plaza surrounded on all sides by *shuks*. Merchants called out their wares urgently, trotting beside them. As they importuned, wheedling them to buy, Alan held out his arm like a shield, to shelter Emmi from them. In one narrow, cobblestoned alley, he paused before a small shop whose slit of window held sparkling glass jars.

"Wait here, Emmi. I shan't be long. You stand here, where I can see you — and don't move!"

The diversity of the crowd flowing past fascinated her: a Greek Orthodox priest with long, thin hair straggling to his shoulders, his black robe sweeping the ground; women, veiled and swathed in black; Arabs in western jackets and pantaloons . . .

Ragged, barefooted urchins, jostling everyone as they darted about, hooted impudently at those who warned them away. One of them approached Emmi and thrust out a bony claw.

"I have only a few German coins," she said, and nervously began fumbling in her purse.

All at once a horde of youngsters swarmed about her with raucous cries. They were revoltingly filthy and their dark eyes held hers with an insolence that frightened her. She edged away, but they drew closer, pressing her to the wall.

Suddenly, a man thrust his way toward her, striking at them with his cane. The boys fled. The man, handsomely dressed in a white linen suit and red fez, bowed and offered Emmi his arm as he addressed her in a language she did not understand. His fleshy, ochre-toned face was as pitted as a sponge, and the pomade on his black hair had a cloyingly sweet smell.

Just then, Alan dashed out of the shop, and the man vanished in the crowd. Alan glowered after him.

"I shouldn't have left you — but I wanted you to have this!" He pressed a bottle of eau de Cologne into Emmi's hands.

"Oh, you shouldn't!" she protested. "Gardenia! It is the scent I am most fond of. You are much too kind to me!"

"It is the other way round," Alan said.

Gripping Emmi's arm, he led her past small booths in which artisans were working — shoemakers, potters, saddlers, silversmiths. They paused to watch a silversmith, who was seated before a hollowed-out carbon block. His swarthy face, with its aquiline features fringed with a black beard, reminded Emmi of Jehiel, the singer of psalms. She watched, completely fascinated by the grace and dexterity of his fingers as he manipulated tiny silver dots into a design and then soldered the design in place with his blowpipe. At his elbow, in a wooden box, lay filigree pins of intricate delicacy.

They walked on, turning into a square dominated by a pale blue mosque embellished with gilt crescents. Opposite stood a café from which a song blared out. Now and then, men stared admiringly at Emmi, and Alan chuckled. "Poor devils. It isn't often they see one like you. I think I'll get you a veil."

"You wouldn't!" she laughed. "Besides, I must meet Avram, or he will worry."

The smile left Alan's face. "Are you in love with Avram?"

"Oh no!" she exclaimed.

"With the American, then?"

"Paul is very nice, but I do not love him."

"With any one else?" he persisted.

"Of course not!" She crimsoned as his grip on her arm tightened.

They came to a street with handsome, modern shops. A placard stood against the mosaic archway of a cinema. Glossy pictures were tacked onto the placard, and she said: "This is an amusing film. I saw it last year."

"Shall we see it?"

"I must not — Avram will be worried."

"I'll keep watch. You won't be late, I promise."

Inside, it was airless and a heavy, sweet perfume made Emmi feel sick. Laughter rose from the dark cavern, and a chorus of voices read aloud the captions that flashed above and below the screen.

Emmi was unaware that Alan was reaching for her hand until his fingers covered hers. They were strong but surprisingly smooth-skinned. She felt pricks of excitement. He whispered into her ear: "Emmi, sweet, you're the nicest thing that's happened to me in this country." She closed her eyes to shut out the images flickering across the screen. She wanted to hear again the sound of his whisper, the utter bliss of his words.

Avram paced the corridor of the Agency office, thinking himself a fool. It was almost an hour past the time set for their return. What if the police siren suddenly went off, clamping a curfew! Emmi would be trapped on the streets — arrested!

He dared not leave without Emmi, but if he delayed starting, it would be dangerous to drive back in the dark!

Earlier, she had phoned, leaving a message that she was on her way to the Agency building. It had relieved his anxiety, but now, as he waited, anger mounted in him. Why hadn't she met him immediately after getting her letter?

Never having been in love, it did not occur to him that possibly the agitation he felt was jealousy.

At last she came. He whipped out savagely: "Where have you been all day?"

Startled, Emmi backed away from the blaze of his eyes. Then she quickened against his anger. "You have no right to shout at me! What I did is my own business!"

Avram flung open the door and strode out of the building. Emmi's face was stony, but when she stepped into the street her chin quivered. They walked to the truck in strained silence.

During the long ride to the *kibbutz*, Emmi felt no consolation in summoning up the pleasures of the day with Alan, for a sense of guilt began edging into each recollection. And then anger welled up in her. She had done nothing wrong or shameful! She felt a sudden loathing for Avram, because he made her feel guilty. And the bottle of eau de Cologne in her hands was like tangible proof of this guilt.

Chapter Six

Ora must be preening herself for the Arab wedding, Paul thought, for she was delaying their departure. He wondered if the settlers resented Noah for choosing him instead of one of them to attend the festivities. But no, when Noah appeared they seized him, rocked him on their interlocked hands and then swung him onto the truck.

"Batlans! Loafers! Is this all you have to do?" Noah scolded, righting himself. But it was easy to see that he enjoyed their affectionate roughing up.

Avram fingered his tie and stretched his neck to ease the unfamiliar encirclement of a collar. His fuzzy dark hair was plastered wetly to his skull, and the blue suit he wore hung baggily on him. Dov, to whom it belonged, had insisted that he wear it; no one at the Arab wedding must say that those of Tel Hashava had not even one good suit among them.

Near the children's section, Emmi was playing ball with Erni. Avram wished she could see how different he looked — she had never seen him dressed this way. They had not spoken to each other for two days — since the Haifa trip.

Where had she been all that day, and with whom, Avram kept wondering. Perhaps he should not have been so harsh with her, but Emmi had to learn that in a *kibbutz* one's pleasure could not be had at a risk to the others.

Of course, silence was a poor way to teach her anything. Emmi was very young, and a newcomer, and he should have explained things to her.

Perhaps if he brought her a little something from the wedding feast, a little anise cake or some confection, it might break the silence between them. Yes, he must remember!

When Ora came out from the row of tents, Paul gave a low whistle. She looked breathtaking in her long green dress with its tight bodice. She wore no make-up. Her black hair, the golden sheen of her skin and her coral lips were all so vivid that make-up would have spoiled the effect.

Dov clucked his tongue with admiration. "Noah, we should go along. The Arabs will go wild when they see her!" and he swung her up to the seat in the cab beside Avram.

At last they were off.

Noah sat on the floor of the truck, his arms locked about his legs. The hot wind kept ruffling his white hair and waving it over a bald patch on his head. After awhile, he began telling Paul about Abu Sa'id and their boyhood together in the Jezreel Valley.

The road climbed. Paul caught a glimpse of the blue waters of the bay. At this height, the ships were toy-size. He wondered if the refugees on the ship had been allowed to land.

The night before — during the general meeting — Avram had hurried into the dining hall, whispered something to Ora, then motioned Dov outside. Paul immediately felt an undercurrent of tension. Later, Shlomo told him that a boat with illegal immigrants had been caught and was being fired upon.

Was Emmi's mother aboard that ship, Paul wondered.

The truck headed south, passing windowless mud huts. An Arab woman plodded down the road with a basket on her head and a baby slung, hammock-fashion across her back. Her loose-flowing black robes fluttered batlike when the truck sped past. Noah waved to her.

"Was Abu Sa'id friendly during the Arab riots?" Paul asked.

"That is always a top question from outsiders," Noah replied with an indulgent smile. "We do not fear the Arabs nearby — only those from across the borders. The village Arabs know we are their friends. They come to our clinics — our feasts — and we go to theirs. We are going to an Arab wedding, are we not?"

Would Hassan ride out to meet her, Ora wondered. What was he like, now that he had been living in England?

They had grown up together and had been fellow students at Jerusalem University. But, in 1945, as soon as the war ended, Hassan had switched to Oxford University. Ora, however, was unable to continue her education. The need to settle new immigrants and train them for work on the land was more urgent, and of greater purpose, than her continued education.

In the beginning, she had tried to keep up with the subjects Hassan was studying; he had sent her books and his lecture notes.

It was very odd, the effect his English-tailored clothes had had on their reunion that first summer of his return. It was as if a stranger, very formal and reserved, had come to visit. And then, the transformation the next day

—when he came out wearing his old shorts and open-neck shirt. There was an emotional pattern to their fare-wells and reunions — the moody silence of their last day together, and the awkwardness and restraint of the first hello.

That summer had seen an anguished leave-taking.

"Let us marry!" Hassan had pleaded the day he left. "You will come to England with me. My father will be pleased to help . . ."

Bur Ora had shaken her head. Hassan was so clever and yet so naïve. Khalil, his father, would not be pleased. In-deed, he had ceased visiting the *kibbutz*. Only Abu Sa'id kept up the old friendship. They had parted with Ora's promise that she would marry him when he returned.

But the Agency had sent her to America on a speak-ing tour and when she returned, he had already left for England.

Would Hassan think her provincial, now that he had lived with sophisticated and educated people? Had he fallen in love with a British girl?

Folding his *abayah* over his knees, Hassan wondered what Ora would think of his costume; he had always worn western clothes. It was odd, the feeling his native dress gave him. At first, he had balked when his father told him to wear it at the wedding; he felt he would be mas-querading. But when he greeted his kinsmen and the guests, he felt less of a stranger among them than he had in the past. It was as if the native garb had removed a barrier between them.

Then, too, the mirror reflected a handsome figure. His embroidered, silken shirt looked quite effective against the white camel's hair *abayah*. And the white *kefiyah*, tied down with a golden coil, made him look older than his twenty years. Ora would laugh at his mustache; it was still only a suggestion of one. He wished it would grow as thick as his eyebrows.

At his table were the British guests, Capt. and Mrs. Ainslee; and the captain's sister, who came dressed as an Arab woman although she should have known that Arab women do not bare their faces or mingle with male guests. The captain's wife was very chic — blonde and pretty, but rather stupid; while old Mrs. Cogswell, a British tourist, seemed to be surprisingly well-informed on Palestine politics. She kept challenging the American journalist, Tad Nourse, on some of his facts. Nourse, however, took it all good-naturedly and amused the guests with tales of his experiences in the land.

Hassan sat facing the courtyard so that he could see Ora as soon as she came. He wondered if the truck had broken down somewhere. Perhaps, he ought to excuse himself and drive down the road a distance. He could then see Ora and be alone with her a few minutes.

What would they do about their love? How could they have a life together, when his people were roused against hers and voices raised for peace were stilled by violence?

More guests were arriving, and the Arab constable in the courtyard was directing the men to the roof terrace and the women to the harem on the lower floor, in the rear. And still there was no sign of the *kibbutz* truck! Nervously, Hassan began chewing his nails, but the vermilion polish tasted bitter and glassy. He cracked his knuckles.

The truck now rattled through an expanse of pasture land that ran in lush green lengths to the hills. A flock of sheep nibbled at the dry stubble left from grain long since gathered. Here and there, small stone houses encircled by neat vegetable gardens were built into the hillside.

A little girl waved and ran alongside the truck. Then, giggling, she turned back. A grizzled old man sat on the stone stoop of a house playing his *rebabi,* his bow sending out a doleful tune.

The houses rose one above the other on the hillside, like large, recessed stone steps. Beyond them stood a blue-domed mosque and, in the distance, a long, crenelated wall. Avram drove straight toward it and an Arab constable opened the gate. With a great waving of his arms, he motioned Avram to drive to the rear.

Horses with bright rugs on their backs, their bridles festive with tassels and blue beads, were drinking out of a trough. Several camels tethered to a pole looked balefully at the truck as it rolled into place nearby. A few military cars, flying the Union Jack, stood parked side by side.

The smell of mutton roasting on an open fire somewhere permeated the courtyard. The settlers walked down a colonnaded passage to a handsomely tiled staircase. Calling, "see you later," Ora turned into a path leading to the rear of the house.

As Paul followed the settlers up the stairs he heard, under the raucous babble of voices, the plaintive strains of an Arab song. The roof terrace was crowded with Arabs sitting in small groups on rugs. At first glance, Paul though they were huddled over in prayer, but then he realized that they were bent over trays of food. They reached out for the meat with their fingers and rolled rice into a ball on their palms and flicked it into their mouths.

There was a great coming and going of men servants carrying platters heaped with meat and rice. Others were preparing coffee on small, handsomely carved inlaid tables — roasting the beans in ladles over charcoal bra-ziers. A subtle aroma of cardamom was in the air.

The settlers stood unnoticed and yet Paul had the odd feeling that everyone had not only seen them, but was exchanging warning glances. Noah's face brightened as Abu Sa'id came toward them.

"Maharba! Welcome! Welcome twice!" the Arab cried, enfolding first Noah and then Avram in a warm embrace. Paul was introduced.

"The friend of my friend is always welcome!" the Arab said. He summoned a boy to fetch his master, and presently a portly man in native dress appeared and bowed to the settlers.

Although his manner was cordial, Paul felt that Khalil Ibn Sa'id el Khoury lacked his father's sincerity. He spoke in Arabic and must have been thanking Noah for something — the old *vattik* deprecated it with a wave of his hands.

"A table will be brought for you," Khalil said.

"We will sit on the floor with the others," Noah re-plied.

"As you wish." Khalil bowed with a constrained smile and, with his father and guests preceding him, followed them to the group from which the old man had risen. The babble of voices ceased abruptly, and Paul felt they were as welcome as a swarm of locusts at a feast. It had been a mistake to come, Noah thought.

The *Mukhtar* of Um Tubas, the village adjoining their newly acquired hill land, eyed him suspiciously. But Arab manners required that he be civil to the guests of his host, and he inquired as to Noah's health. He was a shapeless mass of a man, whose dark fleshy cheeks sagged into rolls of fat under his chin but whose mouth was surprisingly small and shapely.

Haltingly, the conversation was resumed — but it was restrained and guarded talk, with Abu Sa'id inserting a question or a remark whenever there was a lull.

Platters of food were put before them and Noah, who had been warned by Ora to partake sparingly of the rich fare, haplessly eyed the stuffed eggplant and peppers and the succulent meat wrapped in grape leaves. He kneaded the rice and bits of lamb into little balls and flicked them into his mouth, speculating on how much havoc a taste of the spiced watermelon or nuts ground with honey would play with his ulcers.

Later, when a servant held out a basin of water and dish of grated soap, Noah felt he had eaten well, if not wisely.

Abu Sa'id began telling of the happenings in the lower Jezreel, where he lived. "A remarkable thing happened last month. To Ibn el Jabir, a son was born after these many years. But there was no breath of life in him. To us came Sarah, the physician of the Jews, and she gave him breath."

"*Hamdu'illa!*" exclaimed the *Mukhtar* of Um Tubas. "How was this possible, *ya* Abu Sa'id?"

"Before our eyes was this done!" Abu Sa'id continued, after the others murmured their surprise. "She bid us fill hot water in one basin, cold in another, while she breathed hard into the infant's mouth. Then she dipped him, first in one and then in the other basin. The son of Ibn Jabir breathes today."

"*Hamdu'illa!*"

"Thanks to their physicians, our children are being saved," Abu Sa'id pointed up his story.

"Are we not related in Abraham?" asked an old Arab.

"Through Ishmael from Shem," Abu Sa'id nodded. "Is it not Allah's will that we live in peace with our Hebrew brothers? Nowhere in our Holy Book do you find it written that we harm them. Was it not Ibn Sau'ud who said, 'Allah will never forgive the wrong done the Jews'?"

It was an unfortunate remark.

The men were of the Husseini clan — enemies of Ibn Sau'ud. The silence grew frigid as members of the Husseini clan stared hostilely at the settlers.

Addressing himself to Noah, the *mukhtar* said: "It is said that *ma'asha* land has been added to Tel Hashava."

Noah felt the question like a blow at his heart, but he said calmly, "Not even a *dunum* of *ma'asha* land has been bought. Else the Mandatory would not put its seal on the purchase."

"This is a troubled thing, and not of our choosing," the *mukhtar* sighed.

Noah remarked — and to his eternal regret — on the advantages the village of Um Tubas would derive from the road the settlers of Tel Hashava would build, linking the village to the highway. At this, an old Arab who seemed to be dozing as he fingered his prayer beads jerked upright. "The new roads lead to evil ways. We do not want new roads to make it easy for our children to leave the ancient ways of our people."

"We do not want the infernal machines that rush into villages, spreading their foul breath on us," grumbled another.

The *mukhtar* grunted his approval. "That is so. We want no changes. All is foreordained. No man, by impatient striving, can change his fate."

"*Hamdu'illa!*" the old men nodded.

"And progress is fate," Noah said, firmly meeting the cold eyes of the *mukhtar*.

Hassan was worried. Guests kept arriving — some in

cars, others on horseback — but the settlement truck was nowhere in sight. Why had it not come? Was there trouble at the *kibbutz*? The hillsmen from across the border had been active again. He ought to slip away to telephone, but the ladies kept asking him questions.

He was about to excuse himself when Nourse, the American journalist, who had gone below earlier, returned to the table.

"Had a good phone connection?" Capt. Ainslee asked.

"Good connection — bad news," Nourse replied.

"Sorry!" The captain said, tugging at his mustache.

"So are the people who didn't make it," Nourse said.

"Didn't make what?" Hassan inquired.

"Their promised land," Nourse replied dryly.

"Are you referring to last night's incident?" The captain asked.

"Over thirty adults and children were drowned in that incident," Nourse said.

"Oh, how dreadful!" Mrs. Cogswell exclaimed.

"They were warned!" Capt. Ainslee said sharply. "They should have waited for legal permits."

"You ever been in a burning house? I bet you'd never wait for official permission to get out," Nourse said.

The captain muttered something about laws that must be respected while old Mrs. Cogswell repeated, "Dreadful! Shocking!"

Just then, Ora appeared on the landing.

Hassan gave a start. How had he missed the truck? Could this lovely girl really be Ora? She stood surveying the scene with regal poise and he felt himself swelling with pride and love. A wild desire swept over him to hurry her away from the prying eyes of the others.

Ora wondered why Sabba looked so tired. There was a

telltale droop to his shoulders as he bid Abu Sa'id fare-well. She caught Paul's eye and he nudged Avram. They came over to her.

"The *Mukhtar* of Um Tubas insists the land transfer is illegal because some of it is *ma'asha* land," Avram ex-plained. "The *fellaheen* are all worked up and will take it to court."

"That's ridiculous! It wouldn't have been turned over to us if it hadn't been legally cleared," she said.

"Hello Ora!"

Ora wheeled around and caught her breath. "Hassan!"

She felt as though she had shouted his name and that all eyes were on her. But she regained her composure and waited for Hassan to make the next move. He bowed and then introduced the American journalist.

Smilingly, Ora offered Nourse her hand. Hassan stood looking into space while Nourse asked Ora questions about the bride and her guests in the harem. She won-dered how Hassan could stand there, so unresponsive with-out even a glance at her. She knew that he was being discreet in the presence of his kinsmen and yet, how un-like Hassan to be so cautious!

Noah came then, and her heart sank. They were leav-ing and she would not have a moment alone with Has-san! Hassan took a step toward Noah and embraced him. Ora sensed the hostile silence of those Arabs who were near them. Hassan was brave, she thought — embracing a Jew in their midst!

"Come visit us!" Noah said to the journalist, when he was introduced.

"I'd like to . . . how can I get there?"

"I will bring you in my car," Hassan offered.

At this, Ora turned to Nourse with a beguiling smile. Hassan gave her his hand, and a quiver went through her as she looked in his eyes. The gentle pressure of his fingers gripping hers was like a caress. His fingernails, she noticed, were groomed and brightly lacquered. Hers were broken and work-stained. She bit her lips with embarrassment when Hassan noticed them.

When they descended to the courtyard, Ora turned to glance back. Hassan stood leaning over the railing, and his eyes were following her every move.

Chapter Seven

Ora was troubled throughout the ride north to Tel Hashava. Although she had felt a surge of joy that nothing had changed between Hassan and herself, she had an uneasy awareness of a change in him. But she could not define it.

She rationalized the Arab clothes; Hassan had worn them to assure his kinsmen and Arab guests that his two years at a western school had not alienated him from them.

So absorbed was she that she failed to hear Avram's remarks until Hassan's name was mentioned.

" . . . he's learned manners. . . ."

She broke in irritably, "It wouldn't hurt us to learn a few manners ourselves. . . ."

"We were there two hours and in all that time he couldn't tear himself away . . . ."

"Perhaps he didn't see you — or know that we were leaving so soon," Ora snapped. "Incidentally, why did we?"

"Because Abu Sa'id was the only one who wanted us, and even he must have felt that it hadn't been wise to invite us!" Avram retorted.

The lights were on in the office, when they reached Tel Hashava. "Something must be wrong," Noah said.

One look at Chaim, the secretary, confirmed his fears.

"The Agency called. Emmi's mother was on that refugee ship. She was drowned."

They gaped blankly at him. Then all eyes turned to Paul, but he shrank from breaking the terrible news to Emmi.

Finally, Ora said, "I will tell her."

Emmi seemed to feel nothing as Ora told her the news. It was as if her breath, every nerve in her body, her senses, suddenly stood still. Ora spoke bluntly and immediately gave Emmi two pills and some water. Then she undressed her and put her to bed.

Throughout that night and for an eternity of nights Emmi lay motionless, although aware — as from great heights and vast distances — of a succession of faces and whispery voices. One figure succeeded another in the chair beside her cot. She knew dimly that she was in the sick bay.

Noah came. He said nothing, but very tenderly he kept stroking her forehead.

Ora sat with her. She said, "I lost both my parents last summer. I was singing the gay pioneer songs in New York when, here, they were being attacked. The attack lasted forty hours ... Dvora crept miles, with fourteen children, to the German Templar colony ... they didn't open their doors ... she hid the children in the hills ... two were never found ... your Aunt Emmi operated by candlelight when she wasn't firing a rifle ..."

Emmi dreamed. The waters were lapping against her mother's face. She was swimming with the clumsy strokes that had always made them all laugh. Her mother was only a few strokes from shore and Emmi swam out to her. They were near enough now for their outstretched hands to touch. Her own fingers were as stiff as icicles and the moment their hands touched, Emmi's slid away. Her mother fell back silently. And then the waters washed her away.

They brought Erni to Emmi's bedside. He flung himself on her bed with a cry.

"Don't be sick, Emmi," he pleaded. "I will be good — only don't be sick..."

"Mutti is dead, Erni..."

"What does it mean, to be dead?"

"It means one stops being. She will never come..."

"Mutti can't stop being Mutti! She can't! And she will come! She will!" His body shook. He drew away from Emmi and cried out, "You are lying! You are frightening me because I have been naughty!"

The sound of his screams faded away.

Dvora came, the anti-intellectual who had crawled through darkness with the children that night, to a safety that didn't exist.

For a long moment, Dvora and Emmi looked searchingly into each other's eyes. Emmi no longer saw Dvora's homeliness, but a tenderness that completely transformed her. Dvora spoke in Yiddish and Emmi did not understand, but the sorrowing eyes spoke a language that her heart knew. When Dvora left, she put something into Emmi's hand — something hard, in a lace-edged handkerchief. It was a cameo brooch.

And others came, each with a separate sorrow stored deep inside them that reached into Emmi's sorrow. She felt their bond of compassion with her.

Shlomo came, his curly red hair and freckled face brightening up the drab little room. He grinned his apelike grin as he fanned away the flies, and Emmi lay with her eyes shut because they shared no common language and keeping them shut helped to keep out other things, too. When Shlomo left, he put a gargoyle that he had carved out of wood beside Emmi's pillow. It had spidery legs and an elongated head, and its imbecilic grin drew laughter from everyone who saw it. But Emmi did not laugh, for she felt it mocked its own despair.

On the morning of the third day, Dov brought Emmi a bouquet of field flowers still moist with morning dew. He leaned over the bed and saw her eyelids lowered in the pinched, fever-flushed face. He stood a moment, considering, then drew up a chair.

"Emmi, you are awake. Listen to me," he said in German.

Her eyes remained shut.

"When you lose a loved one — you feel yourself lost," he said softly. "You even feel guilty to be the survivor. And whatever you took comfort and joy in before, you find almost sacrilegious to turn to, now.

"But not music, Emmi. Not music."

Her head turned on the pillow. And Dov's tanned, wide-boned face, under his shaggy, strawlike hair remained a blur.

"Not music, Emmi," Dov repeated. "Music is allowed to us to keep us from going mad altogether."

The blur before Emmi settled now and resolved itself into Dov. But his voice lacked its usual, mocking levity. And the ready grin and the teasing look in his eyes were gone. Emmi reached out her hand and Dov took it between his rough palms.

"Once, Emmi," he said, "back there, in my former homeland, something happened. And I said — to hell with life. I thought — my books, my concertina — to whom shall I leave them? So I sat there on the bank where the river cuts our town in two, saying farewell with my concertina. It was as if the music played itself — the last note of one song melted right into the next — refusing to end, just like Scheherazade.

"And I thought, the grave is deep and the dead don't hear; for me, there will never be music again. How, then, can I make an end of it? So here I am, in Palestine. And when the black mood is on me — I take my little stringed soul to the hills. And that is what we will do, my Emmi. I will teach you to find such a healing. Yes? But first, you must want to get well. Yes?"

Emmi's mouth quivered.

It was neither a sleep nor a waking. It was as if, willing herself to die, nothing existed. A spoon at Emmi's teeth sent a sudden shudder through her.

"Eat, my little dove, the broth will give you strength. I made it for you." Bracha's apple-cheeked face with its flat nose was smiling down at Emmi, the large buckteeth protruding over her full lower lip. Emmi turned to the wall. A hand, large as a spade but soft-fleshed, gently turned Emmi's face back.

"Enough of sleep, Emmi. You have slept five full days and nights. Now taste this. The appetite will come with the eating."

"Please, Bracha, I cannot," Emmi said weakly.

"You cannot, because you will not." Bracha's voice was still gentle but her face was now stern. Emmi shut her eyes.

"Emmi, you think no one else has sorrow? Tell me this, how old are you?"

"Seventeen."

"Seventeen!" Bracha gave a grunt. "I was two years

old when I lost my mother — not seventeen! And my father, I lost even before. I used to dream what they looked like — my parents. I even gave them faces. To have *known* one's parents! Oh — how fortunate!

"But in a *kibbutz,* one is never an orphan. One is cared for by all. Always, you have the feeling that you belong. And Emmi, you belong to us all. Everyone sorrowed with you. Avram stayed right here, night after night. He ate his heart out — fearing you would die! And now, you will sip this. I made it just for you. Please, Emmi."

Emmi smiled wanly. The tepid soup slid down her throat, but she could taste nothing.

Paul came to visit, and with him came Jehiel and his little cameo-faced wife, Naami. Emmi did not know how long they had been standing there. Naami smiled shyly. She stood a little behind Jehiel, who was uttering words that sounded like a chant.

There was something noble in Jehiel's dark, aquiline face with its black fringe of beard. Emmi stared into his liquid-soft eyes as if mesmerized by the flow of his chanting. When he fell silent, she looked questioningly at Paul.

"He prayed for your return to health. And he told you that it's wrong to weep yourself into an ailment. It is as if you are denying Him judgment with your tears. We are merely loaned to one another on this earth — and only He in His infinite wisdom knows the right moment for each to return to Him."

Emmi sighed. It was easier than telling Paul that, not being a believer, she could find no consolation in Jehiel's words.

"*Shalom,*" Jehiel said, and with a bow he left Emmi's bedside. Naami, with a timid half-smile, stooped and put something into Emmi's open palm. Then she fluttered away.

"*Todah!*" Emmi murmured.

"They're exquisite!" Paul said, picking up the earrings that slid from Emmi's palm. "How do you feel?"

Emmi shrugged.

"Part of the cure is to wish to be cured."

"Perhaps you are right," Emmi said, tonelessly.

Was it only three weeks since she had come to Tel Hashava? It was useless to look back, for comfort. And there was nothing to look forward to. One black day would follow the next, and the loneliness and the work and the meaninglessness of it all would swallow her life.

Emmi wished she were dead.

Avram came. He sat down clumsily on the white-painted chair next to Emmi's bed and leaned toward her, his big-boned hands spread on his knees. He smelled of grease and of sun. He looked at Emmi with anguished eyes and started to say something, but the words lodged in his throat. He rose and started to leave, stood at the door a moment, then turned back.

"You are not alone, Emmi," he said softly. "You are where you are wanted. You are home."

It was then — for the first time since the news was told her — that she wept.

She was not alone. She was where she was wanted. But she was not where she wanted to be. She was not home.

PART TWO

Chapter Eight

Although Noah thought that the *Mukhtar* of Um Tubas had lied at the wedding when he said *ma'asha* land had been included in the land sale, he nevertheless contacted the Agency to look into the matter. A few days later, he was informed that there had been no complaints from the Arab villagers and that surveyors had already set up boundary markers. Volunteers from the parent *kibbutz* offered to help clear the land, and a few *Haganah* men were detailed to guard the pioneers as they worked.

Ora and Avram were put in charge of the work party. They posted a list of those chosen to work the hill land. No other girl besides Ora was included.

It was not until the moment when they read the list that the settlers believed in the reality of the additional acreage. For two years, it had been a hope pinned on a dream — and now it was actually theirs! The land was not adjacent to Tel Hashava — British Crown land lay in between — but at last they and the Haifa members would be united.

There was great rejoicing that night, and the *hora* was danced until the last star vanished from the sky. The next morning, the Agency phoned to halt all preparations; the *mukhtar* had registered a complaint with the government that *ma'ash*a land had been included in the sale and that the *fellaheen* would defend their communal property with rifles.

"What's wrong?" Ora asked, when she saw Noah's face. "But the sale was final — with the government seal on it!" she cried out, when he told her.

Avram said, "I'll go to Haifa to see what's what..."

"No sense to it," Noah said edgily, pressing his fist to his cheek to ease a toothache. Harnessing these two youngsters to patience was almost as impossible as taming the *khamsin*.

Rolling up the work chart, Ora said bitterly, "They learn fast, those hillsmen! They learned more can be gotten from the British with threats and extortion than by peaceful conduct. The Agency's stopping us will prove how right they are..."

"We waited two thousand years — a few more days won't matter," Noah said, tweaking her ear. "In the meantime, you can begin clearing the north field for the vineyard."

Ora turned away with a grunt of disgust.

The field allotted to the vineyard lay north of the concrete building, beyond the wheat planting and separated from it by a grove of young eucalyptus trees. To the west, Boulder Hill jutted above it in steep shelves, while its eastern border faced the *wadi*, beyond which lay an Arab village.

In the beginning, the settlers had voted to let the field remain fallow as a protective barrier between themselves and the Arabs. But since those in the vicinity had proven friendly these past two years, it was decided to clear it for the vineyard.

Arriving at the field, Ora looked moodily about her.

Where it was bare of stones, the earth was baked to a hard crust and stubbled with cactus bushes. Would there ever come a time when they could buy land in the same way that land elsewhere was bought, Ora wondered. Land that was earth visible and not stone-covered like this field, or like the malarial bog they had already cleared?

The hard physical work of pulling up stones relieved her anger, and presently her thoughts went to Hassan. Nearly two weeks had elapsed since the wedding — why had he not come? Did he need the journalist's visit as an excuse to see her? Then her thoughts went to their Arab friends who had ceased visiting the *kibbutz* since the troubles began. Had they warned Hassan to stay away? But Hassan was not one to be cowed — a threat had always been a challenge to him.

Why then had he failed to come? Avram's cryptic remark came to her mind; Hassan's attentiveness to the British guests at the wedding. She thought of his polished nails, his sleekly groomed appearance in native dress. It conjured up a Hassan who was a stranger to her, and she tried to force him from her mind.

But thoughts of Hassan intruded on everything Ora did, and it appalled her that he took such possession of her inner life when apparently she had ceased to have any meaning in his. She felt a bitterness and resentment that leaped out at anyone who crossed her.

When she came into the dining room for supper, Emmi was at the table for the first time since her illness. The settlers fussed over her, delighted at her recovery. Even Bracha came out of the kitchen to welcome Emmi, urging her to eat heartily to make up for her long fast. Everyone complimented her on how pretty she looked with her hair cut so close to her head.

Dov wanted the cut braids for a wig against future

baldness — and Avram was fascinated by the way her curls, when he touched them, sprang back against her head like little golden springs. Paul greeted her with a hug. But Ora, irked by all this flattering attentiveness, barely glanced at Emmi.

Outside, some children were chasing someone, shouting, *"Yekki! Yekki!"* Erni ran into the dining room, looking around frantically for Emmi. Emmi stood up to call him over to her, but Ora's hand on her shoulder pressed her back.

"Ernst! What are you doing here?" Ora's voice stopped him like a lash.

"I want my sister!"

"Did we come into your dining room when you were eating?"

He shook his head but kept sidling toward Emmi.

"Then you are not to come into ours! Why aren't you in your room, preparing for bed?"

"They call me *Yekki!* They will beat me!"

"No one will beat you unless you provoke him — now go back and behave yourself! Go now!"

Erni fixed his eyes beseechingly on Emmi but she sat with her head lowered. With a sob, he turned and ran out.

"But he is so little — he is so frightened . . ." Emmi said.

"Nonsense! He is not at all frightened!" Ora rapped out. "He uses fear to frighten you. And you make it worse for him by coddling him."

Gently, Avram said: "She is right, Emmi. Ernst must learn not to bully — then he will not need to be afraid."

"But he does not bully them — he — he only defends himself!" Emmi cried brokenly. Then, turning to Paul, she said, "He is not really a bad boy. He was always good at home, but everything here is so — so very different."

"You take him too seriously," Paul said.

"Perhaps you are right," Emmi sighed. Then, after a thoughtful silence, she asked Avram, "But what does *Yekki* mean?"

With an abashed grin, Avram said, "Of course, it is not right, calling him a *Yekki* . . ."

"But what is a *Yekki?*" Emmi insisted.

Avram began stammering a reply when Ora cut in harshly. "A *Yekki* is a two-hundred per cent assimilated German Jew — an anti-Semite — and that's exactly what Erni is!"

"Oh no!" Jumping up, Emmi ran out the room.

"Why didn't you use a bat while you were at it?" Paul flung at Ora with contempt and he hurried after Emmi.

It was not the American's words, but his expression, that stung Ora. No one had ever looked at her with contempt before. She saw it in Dov's eyes, too, and she left the dining room.

Outside, she hurried, almost ran, away from the dwellings and toward the vineyard. She began climbing the craggy heights of Boulder Hill.

Already the clouds were delicately flecked with green and scarlet and saffron. The ridge of hills took on a violet haze, while in the distance the topmost peaks wore crowns of burnished copper. Below, in the *kibbutz*, the lights sprang on like a scattering of stars in mid-air. Ora could see the stubble of wheat they had harvested and nearby, a low growth of dark green in the field they had seeded to barley. In the dusk, the young eucalyptus trees looked like fuzzy cones.

Somewhere below, Dov was playing his concertina and

this completed the scene in all its idyllic beauty, for Ora. She was seized with such love of the land that she threw out her arms and then folded them across her chest as if she were hugging it all to her.

Israel! It was a small fragment of a country but it was the beating heart of the world, its immortal soul, for. here had arisen the eternal truths that shaped man's destiny.

It was a parched land, a famished land, a land that "devoureth the inhabitants thereof." It was sick with every ailment that beset mankind, and it was poor with a poverty that crushed those who did not defy it. The land contained the whole meaning, the very essence, of her being.

She need not have gone abroad to discover its obsessive hold on her. But she knew with an inexorable certainty that to live for this land she was destined to die for it. She stood locked in this embrace with the land and then, suddenly, the ecstasy left her and her arms dropped heavily to her sides. She turned away and sat down on the flat lip of a boulder.

People like Emmi were wrong for the Land! Ora thought.

Only those belonged who had a reverence for it — not those who came seeking a temporary refuge from the storms abroad. Only those belonged whose every atom of being pulled them homeward to the Land. Only those belonged who had the stamina to risk life in order to bring life to this ravaged land.

And Emmi was weak — not only weak, but she *resented* being here! Resented! This was an affront to those pioneers who had redeemed the barren wastes with their lives, to those who had braved bullets and the devouring sea to reach home.

Presently, the crushed look on Emmi's face came to Ora and she felt a twinge of remorse. Emmi was young, only seventeen. It was not her fault that she was so immature. Abroad, Ora had observed, one is neither an adult nor a child at seventeen. There, seventeen-year-olds had adult desires coupled with a childish lack of responsibility. Ora had been appalled by it.

Here, in the Land, there was no such confusion, no such irresponsibility. At seventeen, you understood and accepted the principles of the community; you shared the work, you shared the benefits and you shouldered a rifle to defend all this. Yes here, at seventeen, life very definitely made you an adult!

The trouble was that everyone coddled Emmi — Noah, Bracha, Paul, Avram — even Dov! Paul had taken on the role of chief protector, defending Emmi against *her*, Ora! And remembering Paul's look of contempt, anger flared up in Ora again. She picked up a stone and flung it at the darkening valley.

Running downhill, Ora's shoe caught in a tangle of weeds and she stumbled and fell. She knelt down to free it, tearing at a long, wire-strong vine. It was as if an octopus had closed its tentacles over the shoe, enmeshing it. It was an ingil. Then a laugh that was like a wild cry broke from her.

Noah must have wished it there for her to stumble over, and be warned. Often enough he had told her that her temper was a wild growth, like an ingil — a plant that has no roots of its own but sends out tentacles to feed on other plants and trees. Then, sucking out their life juices, it strangles whatever it twists about. The ingil in Ora was her own wild, uncontrollable temper.

At last, she wrenched her shoe free. In a subdued mood,

she walked slowly back to the settlement thinking, yes
— she had behaved shamefully toward Emmi. It really
was not Erni's undisciplined conduct that had provoked
her outburst — it was jealousy of Emmi's popularity!
And Ora had snapped at the others that day as if it was
their fault that Hassan had failed to come.

There must be something lacking in herself, Ora
thought, which men sensed and which made them indif-
ferent to her. The thought dejected her unbearably because she knew she could do nothing about it. She was
what she was — a patriot.

But she must try to be more tolerant toward Emmi.
And more civil to the American. After all, he was "pulling his weight" along with the others; he could have
asked for light work, but chose the most arduous. And
because of this, she must regard him with the same respect and consideration as she did the others.

Late the next afternoon, Noah called to her from the
window of the office. "Ora! Come in!"

Reluctantly, she went into the office. Nourse, the American journalist, greeted her at the door and even before
she saw Hassan, she knew that he was there. She was
only vaguely conscious of shaking hands with Nourse because of the wild leapings of her heart and the dizziness
she felt, on seeing Hassan.

Avram and Paul followed Ora into the office and as
they greeted the visitors, Ora saw that Hassan was handsomely dressed in a white linen suit. She felt self-conscious about her own appearance and ran her fingers
through her hair. Straightening her blouse, she could
feel a rent at the shoulder, and bit her lip with vexation.

Eager for them to see the *kibbutz,* Noah hurried his
guests out and bubbled with enthusiasm as he showed
them about. The journalist, Ora thought, was unim-

pressed by what he was seeing but he seemed drawn to Noah, and for this she was ready to forgive the sarcastic appraisal in his eyes.

Avram took possession of Hassan, wanting to know about their mutual Arab friends in the Jezreel Valley. Ora walked silently beside Paul. She stumbled over a plank at the construction site for the new barn and Paul threw his arms about her, steadying her. Hassan frowned. He was jealous! Ora felt so elated about this that she smiled at Paul.

"This will be a palace for our livestock," Noah said, and described the barn yet to be built.

"But you already have a barn," Nourse observed.

"It is wooden — a temporary one. Our cows are our treasure. To give us our needs, we must give them theirs. After all, they are not Zionists..." Noah chuckled.

Laughing, Nourse slapped the old *vattik* appreciatively on his back.

Would they never have a moment alone together, Ora wondered, as children and settlers joined them. The friendliness of the journalist put them all at ease, and the settlers fired questions at him which kept Paul and Avram busy interpreting. Hassan edged away from the crowd and signalled Ora to join him.

Silently, they walked to the end of the cement building while Ora fought back an impulse to ask why he had not come sooner. The laughter and the voices of the crowd faded as Ora and Hassan reached the last of the *kibbutz* buildings. Suddenly, Hassan reached out and swung Ora to him, kissing her on the mouth.

For a moment, she clung to him. Then she wrenched herself free. "Why didn't you come sooner?" she demanded.

Hassan cupped her face with his hands. "The same

Ora — lips of honey and eyes of fire. How could I come sooner? The wedding festivities lasted through the week and more guests arrived. I could not offend my kinsmen by leaving. The last of them left only yesterday."

The answer failed to ease her hurt. He could have come — had he wanted to be with her. Obedience to his father's wishes had never before kept him from following his own.

"I wished them all gone, Ora, so that I could come to you," he said, putting his arm around her waist. She held herself stiffly away from him. Shouts of children at play rang out, and she said, "We may be seen!"

"Does it matter? Noah and Avram know that I love you."

His dark, intense face, with the wild sweep of brows that met at the hawk-shaped nose, was exactly as she remembered it — and yet she felt a change in him. "Hassan, have you seen Tewfik?" she finally asked, regretting the question as soon as she had spoken. She wanted this moment to be utterly theirs, and untroubled. And Tewfik, their friend and former classmate, had become an enemy.

The smile vanished from Hassan's face. "Yes, I have."

"What made him change? What made him go from unity with us to enmity? Tewfik — of all people!"

Hassan avoided Ora's eyes and kicked idly at a small stone. There was an irritable edge to his voice when he replied, "You know very well why. He thinks the flood of immigrants makes unity impossible — that the Zionists are taking over the country, displacing the Arabs. Only militant action ..."

Don't press him — not now, Ora pleaded with herself; it is too soon ... but I must know where he stands

. . . I must! Before she could restrain herself, she blurted out, "And what do you think?"

She fixed him with a look that was at once a challenge and a plea, as if willing him with every part of her being to say only what she wanted to hear. He held her stare a long moment and then said in a low voice, "I want peace for our love."

With a cry, Ora flung her arms about him. "Hassan — I was so afraid!" He tipped her face back and kissed it. "But how could it be otherwise — between us?"

A flamelike radiance came to her face and she smiled warmly and movingly at him. "Ora, when you smile like that, I am lost," Hassan said. He took her in his arms.

"You will be — if you don't get back," she laughed. "By now, Noah must have exhausted the poor journalist." They began retracing their steps. "Tell me about Oxford. Did you miss me at all?" Ora asked.

"You spoiled it for me with the girls," he said, lacing his fingers through hers. "They lack something that only Ora has. They are beautiful, yes, but it was like trying to warm myself at a *picture* of a fire. Or, if they were intelligent, they lacked my Ora's sharp wit."

"You sound as if you had a harem."

"A Moslem is entitled to four wives, legally."

"I wish you joy with all of them," she teased.

"I need only one to give me joy." Then, suddenly, the bantering mood left him and he tightened his hold on her arm. "The American — he is quite handsome and intelligent. Nourse told me he's here on a Harvard Fellowship."

"Yes, he is quite intelligent," Ora admitted.

"He is in love with you. I could tell back there, when he threw his arms around you."

Ora restrained a chuckle. Paul — in love with her! That dry stick who went around jotting down psychological notes on everyone!

The journalist was still surrounded by the settlers as Ora and Hassan drew near. Noah was as exuberant as ever but Nourse seemed tired. His shoulders sagged and he had the strained look of one who had listened to tales of woe beyond his saturation point.

"Let's step on it!" he called out when Hassan appeared.

Ora was about to ask when he was coming again when Hassan said, "My father and I are returning a kinsman's visit, but I will come as soon as we return."

There was a pleasant exchange of farewells, for the journalist had won the settlers' affection. Hassan and Noah embraced and Noah asked Hassan to bring his grandfather with him on his next visit.

Hassan's eyes, as he started the engine, smiled at Ora with a secret message. She nodded and then ran lightheartedly to her tent, her whole being flooded with love for everyone. She went over to Emmi, and startled her with a hug.

Chapter Nine

 From the storehouse where she now worked, Emmi heard the truck rattling toward the road and she ran out, waving a list. Avram drew to a stop and leaned down to take the paper. He gave a whistle when he saw the number of items on it.

"Soap? Toothpaste? Tell them to use salt for their teeth. It's better for their gums — and cheaper." His teeth flashed white when he smiled. In the glare of the sun, his eyes squinted so that Emmi could only see the dancing lights in the dark pupils. His fuzzy hair stood upended in the hot wind and Emmi wished he would cut it short. Short hair would make him look less — well — less rough.

"If it's not too late when I return, I will take a walk up Boulder Hill. Come along, if you like," Avram said casually.

"Oh, I would like to very much!" Emmi cried eagerly, and when he smiled, she added, "May I take Erni?"

"Why not? Let's take all the children," he said irritably, and drove away.

She watched the truck until it vanished in a cloud of dust, thinking, that she should not have asked to take Erni. Alone with him, I could explain about that day in

Haifa . . . that I did not meet him earlier only because I wanted to be alone . . . that I met Alan quite by accident. He will believe me — and we will be friends.

Oh, why is life so complicated by trifles, she sighed. If I hadn't been ill, Avram might still be angry with me! Surele, the nurse, had told her how Avram had taken over her night watches during those crucial nights of her illness. Yes, she must explain herself when they walked to the hill; she owed him that.

She returned to the storehouse, a one-room hut that stood between the barn and the children's section of the cement house opposite the row of dwellings.

It was like no other shop Emmi had ever seen. The shelves held a variety of items — shirts, tousers, shorts, socks, underclothes, writing paper, shaving brushes and other things. The rear window looked out on the barn construction site and the chicken run. In the middle of the room stood a table heaped with linen and clothes to be mended.

Five days before, when Emmi had first been assigned to work there, the novelty of the shop had fascinated her. The settlers simply asked for an item and it was given to them — without money or a credit slip or even a record being made of it!

At first, Emmi had done the mending in the laundry. The soiled linen and clothes were heaped around four tubs and the girls kept up a noisy chatter as they scrubbed away, splashing the soapy water everywhere. They had been friendly, but they spoke in Yiddish and communication with them was difficult. Emmi understood enough, though, to know that they were gossiping about Ora and the Arab.

One of the girls hinted that the Arab was Ora's lover; she had seen them slip off by themselves. Another resented this slur on Ora, and a quarrel broke out. Their wrangling over Ora, whom she detested, set Emmi's nerves on edge and thereafter she took the mending to the storehouse.

Thus, for five hours daily she worked alone and while she preferred this to the noise in the laundry, there were times when she felt quite lonely. Then, too, the nature of her work made no demands on her mind so that, inevitably, her thoughts pulled her back to Erlangen — into the familiar world of yesterday. She remembered those days that held a particular happiness — her piano recital, the outings with Gunther, the trips to England with the family when she was a child.

Sometimes, she would relive the day spent in Haifa with Alan, recapturing the thrill of being with him — from the moment she met him in the post office, until that whisper, "Emmi, you are the nicest thing that's happened to me here." She always ended with this, for afterward came the ride back with Avram in the hurt and angry silence.

It was only mid-morning, but already the heat had become unbearable. The blouse Emmi was mending lay crumpled in her hands like a damp rag. She smoothed it out and frowned with self-disgust at the botch she had made. She began to rip the mending out when she saw that the blouse was Ora's. She had a mad urge to tear it to shreds.

Oh, how she loathed her. Ora had apologized for her conduct and had even hugged Emmi the day Hassan had visited, but Emmi felt she would never forgive her for her heartless treatment of Erni in the dining hall. Why was Ora so insensitive to Erni's special needs?

He was only a child, unhappy and confused in this alien land. Everything worked on his nerves — his fear in the night when the searchlight swept its beam into his room like a ghostly finger, tearing him out of his sleep; the howling of the jackals; the teasing of the children when he wet the bed. He had lost everything dear and familiar, and needed love and attention to balance his loss.

Emmi was unaware that she was not alone until she felt a hand at her forehead. It was Noah's.

"Are you not well, Emmi?"

"The heat..." she murmured.

"If that is all, it will soon pass. Of two things we are always certain — that the *khamsin* will come and that it will go. Otherwise, how do you feel?"

Smoothing out Ora's crumpled blouse, Emmi smiled wryly. "Quite well, thank you. I have resigned myself."

Noah shook his head. "To resign oneself is to accept negatively. And that is not good. In fact, it is not good at all."

It was the closest Noah had ever come to a rebuke with her, but he said it in so fatherly a tone that Emmi took his hand and held it. His grip had a gentle strength and she felt it pervading her, lifting her spirits. The feeling lingered even when he left.

It was wonderful, the power Noah had to lift her out of her dejection. She took Ora's blouse, ripped out the messy seam and, when she finished sewing, gave a nod of approval.

Dov stood in the doorway with something dark rolled under his arm. His hair looked like sun-bleached straw over his tanned, wide-boned face. His blue eyes twinkled mischievously.

"Emmi, how many feet I have?" Dov spoke German fluently but preferred to speak English, which he spoke poorly.

"Two, I think." She glanced at his feet.

"So! Is here two feet?" Thrusting his leg into shorts Emmi had mended, he hopped, storklike, around the room. She had sewn the two leg parts together! He looked so comical hopping about on one leg that Emmi burst into laughter.

"Emmi, I will make with you an exchange! You be my friend and I will not tell nothing, yes?"

"But I am your friend!"

"You say so, but you do not feel so. Here, everybody is friends with each other but you — you smile, but like from another world." He went over to Emmi, took her sewing from her and held her hands. His face was serious.

"Emmi, we are people like you, also from another world," he said, speaking in German now. "We came strangers one to the other, but here we became sisters and brothers. But you — you are still a stranger to us."

She turned her eyes away from his intense, questioning look. "I do not feel myself a stranger with you — or Paul," Emmi said.

"Good! Then you will please do more than smile at me. You will come for walks with me and you will tell me things."

"Oh, I would like that very much — but you are always so busy! Rina — and Miriam — and all the other girls . . ."

"Little one! You are jealous! Good!"

"But I am not jealous — only — you are so very popular — the girls will think I am taking you away from them . . . ."

"You will be taking me away only from myself, and that will be good! So we have made a bargain, yes? We are friends?"

"Yes! Oh yes!" she agreed eagerly.

"Remember!" he wagged his finger and then hurried away.

Outside, Miriam, the kindergarten teacher, was coming along the road with her five little charges. Emmi could see Dov pausing to chat with her. Then he swung a child onto his shoulder and went galloping down the road. Their mingled laughter trailed off in the distance, but the smile lingered on Emmi's face.

Dov always put her in a good mood; and Paul put her in a thinking mood; and Noah gave her the feeling of being lovingly shielded, and Avram — Avram made her feel guilty about Alan.

Early that afternoon, Emmi heard Avram's truck rattling past the storehouse again. Why had he returned so soon? Had he been attacked? Dreadful things were happening in the country. In the British papers that came to the *kibbutz*, she had read of Arab riots that took place whenever a ship with refugees docked, of Arab attacks on Jewish villages, of ambush and sniping on the highways.

It was all very frightening. Last week, when she had spoken of this to Paul, he had chided her for being so childish. Had she not seen Arab visitors at Tel Hashava? And had not Avram and Dov taken the tractor that very week to the Arab village across the *wadi*, to plow its fields?

Emmi thought now of the Arab and his wife who had brought their child to the sick bay when she was ill. The child had been mauled by a dog. Surele had treated the wounds, and the parents had sat on the floor all through the night. Bracha had brought them food and had sat with them, talking in Arabic. At first, they had been shy, but Bracha's warmth had drawn them out and before long, the three were chattering like old friends.

The next morning, the child, covered with bandages, was taken home. A few days later, the child's father returned carrying a kid as a gift. From where Emmi was sitting, she could see the little animal tied to a length of rope, frisking about outside the barn.

It was, as Paul had said, childish of her to be frightened. She was seventeen years old and should be mature. She should accept things philosophically — as they are — and not go off dreaming of how she wanted them to be. You must begin by controlling your emotions, Emmi chided herself. She gave a violent start as Erni burst into the room, shouting, "Emmi! They're here!"

"Who is here?"

"Karl — the German constable! And Alan! Come quick!" Seizing her arm, he yanked impatiently.

As Avram led Sergeant Cassidy to the truck, he told of the attack in his dry, matter-of-fact tone. Noah and Ora listened with gloomy faces; it was a portent of things to come.

"Must have been the Bedouins," Cassidy said, examining a bullet hole that had splintered the truck roof. "Nobody from these parts can shoot a moving target at the distance you were."

"Somebody's been training them to set their gunsights for long-range shooting, to cries of 'Heil Hitler,'" Ora put in.

"Why can't I get a permit to carry a rifle?" Avram asked.

"We would have to give the Arabs permits, and then all hell would break loose," Sgt. Cassidy answered.

"The others don't need permits. They've got the rifles," Ora retorted.

Cassidy ignored her remark. The grown Ora was even sassier than she had been as a child. He said irritably, "This partition business at the United Nations — all the immigration — the Arabs go bloody wild about such things ..."

"They wouldn't if they weren't stirred up," Ora said.

Cassidy put a scowl on his face — his official expression. The settlers tensed expectantly, feeling ill-at-ease, now on their guard with an old friend.

"Noah, illegal immigrants are being slipped into border settlements. I have to make an inspection."

"A duty is a duty," Noah said.

When they reached the dwellings, Cassidy fixed Noah with a searching look. "Noah, if you say there are no illegal refugees here, I will not make the inspection. But you must say so in God's name."

Noah met his glance calmly and steadily. "In God's name I say there are no illegal refugees here."

Outside the dining hall, they caught a glimpse of Bracha before she stepped away from the window. For once, her toothy grin failed to welcome the Britisher. "Bracha is offended that you did not stay for tea last time," Noah said. "She thinks you have given us up."

"You know the captain's orders ... no socializing," Cassidy said. But he followed Noah into the dining hall where a smell of fried onions permeated the air. Cassidy brightened — potato pancakes!

Bracha came in carrying a loaded tray. She nodded unsmilingly to Cassidy as she put a plate heaped with golden pancakes before him. "I did not make this just for you, Cassidy," she said, with an offended air. "I was making them for supper. Lately, you have no time for us — like in the old days. You have become more of a policeman than a friend."

"No time for friends, these days," he retorted.

"Noah! Quick — my Rosa!" a woman cried agitatedly.

"That Dvora!" Noah clucked his tongue as he ran out.

"What's wrong with Rosa?" Cassidy asked.

"She is past due to calve," Bracha replied.

"Such a to-do! You'd think it was a human!"

"To Dvora it is," Bracha said. "And to us, too! We lost our last cow when she calved. What a treasure for us, if this one lives!" She sighed, visualizing a barnful of newborn calves.

"Will another cow buy you a new dress?" Cassidy asked.

Self-consciously, Bracha smoothed out her worn cotton dress. "That does not matter, now. Other things are more important. But next year ... if ... we live .."

"I won't be here then," Cassidy said

The blood drained from Bracha's face. "What do you mean?"

"We'll be out by then ... we're giving up the mandate."

Bracha gaped as if a prop had suddenly been pulled from under her. "Cassidy, you would not leave Palestine."

"Now, what would I be doing in this bloody country after His Majesty's forces quit it!"

"Join us," Bracha said. "Farming is better than police work."

"You're the daft one. Capt. Ainslee says I'm half Jew already — the saints preserve us."

"You don't have to be one, to join us."

"I thought you were the daft one when you were little — you've not grown up to any sense at all." The stack of pancakes had vanished now, and the line in the jam pot had receded to the bottom. Cassidy wet his fingers and wiped away all traces of the meal from his mustache.

"That was a good tea, Bracha." He looked at her a

long moment and then said, "You're a grown girl. It's time you got married."

"I'm still waiting...," she giggled.

"You've grown too bold, my girl." A blob of jam had trickled down his jacket. Bracha rubbed at it with her scarf and then gave a quick polish to the silver buttons.

"For all your rum talk, you're a good girl," he said. He raised his hand to touch her cheek but dropped it again. Then he strode out of the room with a frown.

Bracha stood at the window, watching the stocky figure walk briskly down the road. With a deep sigh, she picked up the dishes. Wouldn't it be wonderful if the British left? she thought. But not Cassidy — not her Cassidy.

Emmi saw the blank look on Alan's face and she flushed — he did not like her hair cut short! "You don't like it?" she asked.

"I guess I'll get used to it. You look fine!" he said then. "Makes you look like a cute little girl."

"I don't feel like one," Emmi said.

"I shouldn't wonder. Terrible thing, losing your mother." He fumbled for something in his pocket, then brought out a small onyx brooch.

"Oh, that's the one we saw at the silversmith's. It's very beautiful!" she exclaimed.

"I bought one like it for my mother," Alan said. "This one is for you."

"Oh no! I cannot accept it!"

"Of course you can. Here, let me pin it on you."

Erni saw Alan bending over his sister, and he wanted to shout with joy. The things he had thought about would surely happen now. Emmi would marry the Britisher, and they would all live in England! Of course, he preferred that she marry Karl, the constable — who was German — but Emmi did not fancy him at all.

Watching them, at first Erni did not hear Karl speak. " . . . and are you a good Jew now?" he was asking.

Erni stiffened. "I am a German!"

"And the new one who came — is he a German, too?"

"I haven't seen a German," Erni said. "The ones who come from Haifa for the Sabbath are all Jews. I do not bother with them."

"Ach — a pity! I can see you are not happy here." Erni was about to confide his hopes about Emmi and Alan to Karl but Karl reached for a newspaper in the pickup and began reading. Erni felt dismissed.

"That was a close call," Alan remarked, as Avram went over to greet him. The windshield directly in front of the steering wheel was cracked and there was a small hole in the middle.

"I ducked just in time," Avram grinned.

"Look, Avram, isn't this beautiful?" Emmi said, holding out the brooch. "Alan gave it to me."

Glancing briefly at the pin, Avram said, "Yemenite work. They are very artistic with metal."

"We saw it in one of those *shuks* in Haifa," Alan said. "Emmi seemed taken by it but she wouldn't let me buy it for her."

"Haifa?" Avram's face tightened. Suddenly, it was all clear to him. Emmi had been with Alan that day! Oh, she was a crafty one — pretending that she just wanted to be alone — and he had been frantic with fear . . .

Emmi paled at the look Avram gave her.

Cassidy was heading for the pickup, and Alan, with only a brief smile, hurried over to it. Suddenly, Emmi regretted accepting his gift. Surely he must think her forward to have accepted a gift from one who was little more than a stranger.

Avram's face, as he walked away, looked very angry. Erni started to follow Avram, but Emmi stopped him.

"But he said we were going to Boulder Hill!"

"We will go — some other time," Emmi said edgily.

"Emmi, has the German come yet?" Erni asked.

"What German?"

"The new one — the one Karl asked me about . . ."

"We're the only Germans here!" she snapped irritably.

The German came that Friday, with the Haifa members. Although everyone greeted him as if he was an old settler, Emmi had an odd feeling that he was a newcomer to the country.

Everything about him, from his clean-shaved, narrow, elongated head to the precise manner in which he spoke, proclaimed him a German, a kinsman. He was skeleton-thin with a tissue of skin stretched tautly over his bones. His eyes were deep-set and darkly shadowed.

He was sitting with Noah, and Emmi walked past them several times, hoping to be noticed and introduced. And yet she dreaded meeting him, fearing that she might not be able to restrain herself from asking if he had been on the same ship with her mother. It would be like asking him if he were here illegally.

When she wasn't speculating about the newcomer, she fretted over Avram. He had been ignoring her and she was racked with contrition. She wanted desperately to explain how it happened that she had spent that day in

Haifa with Alan. But Avram's manner froze her into silence.

The mending went poorly the morning after the Sabbath. Emmi pricked her finger and smeared blood over a shirt. It was not until she heard a cough that she looked up. The newcomer — the German — stood before her. She jumped to her feet.

"I am told one gets work clothes here," he said, slurring the words in the thickness of his speech. He limped as he drew nearer to the work table, and Emmi saw that there was a gash in his lower lip and an emptiness where his front teeth should have been. She stiffened, to keep from shuddering. Back "there," when people returned after a long disappearance, they had the same black gaps in their gums, the same cracked lips, the same ashen, bony faces.

"What size, please?" she asked, forcing a smile.

"It does not matter, as long as they cover my bones," he replied. He smiled wryly.

Emmi looked for a shirt and pair of denim trousers on the shelves.

"Noah told me you are from Erlangen," the German said softly.

Wheeling around, Emmi asked in a high-pitched voice, "Are you, also?"

"Close enough," came the reply. "Nürnberg."

"Oh!" she exclaimed, clasping her hands in delight. "We used to go there often! To concerts, museums, Altstadt, Albrecht Dürer's..." She rattled off the names of different places, her excitement mounting with each remembered name.

"...and then Mutti would take us to the markets under the Pegnitz bridges. Oh — we loved Nürnberg!

Once, when I was very young, my music teacher took me there to visit Frau Cosima Wagner..."

Emmi stopped speaking. The thin gash of the newcomer's mouth had compressed suddenly, and his eyes held a bitterness that chilled her. She felt sick with guilt at her thoughtlessness, and tears came to her eyes.

But the anguished look left his face and a smile twisted across it. "That must have been a long time ago — before..."

"Yes... before... before..." she said hoarsely.

"Before we were gathered into Noah's ark." A wistful smile crossed his face — one that went with the remembered phrase, "What can't be cured must be endured." It was a facial uniform, that smile. Emmi knew it well.

The newcomer took his bundle and limped out. At the door, he turned and bowed.

Emmi had a strong feeling that she had met him before.

That night, when Emmi had finished her evening meal, she saw the newcomer sitting with Noah. She felt an urge to speak to him; there was so much to say, so much to ask about. Did he know her father, Eric Leiter, the famous jurist? It would be wonderful just to talk about her father, Emmi thought. At home, she had loved it whenever Mutti talked about him. Mutti had never made it seem as if he were dead — only absent. Maybe, if she heard her father's name spoken aloud by another, it would again seem as if — he were only absent.

The newcomer was engrossed in talk with Noah but as Emmi approached, he looked up and a warm smile mellowed his face. She was overcome with shyness and, returning his smile, she walked quickly to the door.

Paul took Emmi's arm as she came out and they

strolled down the road together. She asked him about the newcomer.

"He is the famous penologist, Dr. Friedrich Vogel . . ." Paul said.

"But, of course!" Emmi cried excitedly. "My father knew him! We had his books! They were bound in leather and father let me wax the covers! He even visited us. Oh! I must tell him." She turned to go back but Paul stopped her.

"No you don't! I shouldn't have told you! Forget that I did, you understand? He is to be known only as Shimon. That means, "the Lord has heard." It comes from the word *shema,* which means "to hear." Why aren't you in the Hebrew class?"

But Emmi was not listening now. A wonderful feeling had come over her — as if something extraordinary were happening. It was as if — almost as if — her father were about.

"Hey, come down from the clouds!" Paul said, shaking her arm. "Why aren't you in Hebrew class?"

"I don't feel like going tonight," Emmi said then.

"Learning by mood is no way to learn," Paul admonished.

She smiled thinly. "Avram is angry with me."

"So what? Is that any reason for staying away from class?"

They had reached the school hut. Through its open window, Emmi could see a cloud of midges, like black gauze, swarming around the naked bulb that hung from the ceiling. Avram was pacing the floor, a book in his hand. Emmi watched him until he moved out of sight.

"Perhaps I had better go to class. Perhaps I can see Avram afterward, and talk to him. We've had — a misunderstanding."

"Good idea, Emmi," Paul said.

She braced her shoulders and hurried to the hut as though she wanted to get to the classroom before her eagerness left her. At the door, she turned and smiled at Paul. He waved.

Shlomo's gargoyle face was lowered over a book, but he glanced up when Emmi came into the room and patted the empty space next to him on the bench.

When Avram looked at her, Emmi felt the blood rushing to her head. He was explaining a rule of syntax and did not cease talking as their stares met and held. Then he went over to her and put his own book, before her. "Tenth line, Emmi," he said. He spoke dryly, but Emmi caught a smile on his face as he turned away.

Chapter Ten

A shaft of light shimmered on the ground before the open flap of Paul's tent. He had not lit his lamp, and Shlomo was in the Hebrew class. Paul frowned; he was eager to get on with his notes and was in no mood for visitors.

"*Shalom,* Paul," Dov said. He was lying on Shlomo's cot. A valise and his concertina stood at the opening of the tent. Paul tripped over it and swore.

"I exchanged places with Shlomo," Dov announced.

"So I see," Paul said, irked that he had not been consulted. Shlomo had proved himself a compatible tent-mate. Although talkative, he had the consideration to be quiet when Paul was typing. With Dov, whose moods ranged from an unbroken silence to an unbroken patter of talk or song, Paul felt apprehensive about his research.

"They put Shimon in my tent," Dov offered by way of an explanation. "He doesn't snore. He doesn't even sleep. He just lies awake and stares at the sky. And he won't let me close the flap — he can't stand being closed in — said he had enough of it in Nazi prisons. So I asked Shlomo to change with me."

Paul nodded glumly. Dov was intelligent and witty and he liked him. But not as a tent-mate.

"I think I'll drop in on the *kumsitz,*" Dov said. He

swung himself off the cot, reached for his concertina and left — in one supple, unbroken movement.

Paul picked up a shoe that Shlomo had overlooked. Dov poked his head into the tent again, grinning.

"I forgot to ask — can I move in with you?" He ducked as, with a burst of laughter, Paul flung the shoe at him.

Paul barely had time to set up his typewriter and sort out his notes when Dov was back. He frowned. If this was to be a nightly routine, he had better apply for a separate tent. "The *kumsitz* over already?" he asked dryly.

"For me it is," Dov said irritably, flinging himself on the cot. Suddenly, he sat upright and said excitedly, "They're mad! You know what they were discussing? What *kibbutz* to go to for the High Holy Days! Think of it! It's all that Jehiel's doing! He'll turn them into rabbis yet!"

"What's wrong with that? I plan to go, too," Paul said.

Dov gaped at him as if he had taken leave of his senses. Then, with a grunt of disgust, he undressed and pulled the blanket over his head.

Paul slid the typewriter under his cot and began to work on his notes.

Dov was definitely a puzzle. Paul simply couldn't find a psychological clue to explain him. At first, Dov had struck him as a shallow egotist. Later, however, despite his glib, spicy talk and easy comraderie, he thought there were concealed depths in him.

Sometimes, Dov was boisterously gay. Other times, however, he appeared so dejected that Paul caught a look in his eyes that seemed to reflect thoughts he couldn't live with. At such times, Dov would take his concertina to the far end of the *kibbutz* land and abandon himself to playing wildly gay songs — or sad pieces that tore at one's heart. And when he returned, Paul thought his face looked as spent as if he had been on a long, steady drinking bout.

Unlike the others, who willingly told Paul about their background, Dov was uncommunicative about his. Paul sensed that he not only was trying to blot out the past (as when he would shrug off a personal question with a wisecrack) but that he refused to admit to himself the extent to which the past was affecting his present moods.

Dov's cynical reply to an idle remark convinced Paul of this. The two had been discussing girls, and Dov said, "Girls! Tricksters! They fall in love with you as you are and then start making you over. The girl I loved back home was a better human being than I was or ever will be, but she . . ." and he lapsed into silence.

"Why don't you send for her?" Paul asked.

"The dead don't travel," Dov said, with his twisted grin. Then he reached for his concertina and began playing. He sang so softly that Paul had to strain to hear the words.

"The stormy days carry us, each is a wave,
Driving us nearer the shore of the grave . . ."

Listening, Paul thought that life for Dov had ceased to have any real purpose and that in coming to Palestine, he had chosen its farthest outpost, Tel Hashava, more out of a sense of destiny than dedication.

Dov did not prove to be as annoying a tent-mate as Paul had anticipated, but his conduct revealed contradictions in his make-up that were puzzling. He had declared himself an atheist but when a few settlers went off for the High Holy Days, he gave them the last of his cash reserve to buy prayer books that were needed.

And it was Dov who began building the tabernacle for the *Succoth* holiday. He kept up a din about one big dwelling for all when they got the hill land and yet until Shimon came, he had lived alone in a tent.

At meetings, he resisted responsibility. Yet, when he volunteered to do anything, he worked at it as if his very life depended on its completion.

He had been working on the *succoth* he had promised Jehiel for the Feast of Tabernacles. He worked at it every evening when he came back from the fields, bolting down his food and nagging his "team" — Paul, Avram and Shlomo — to hurry with theirs.

That day, which was Friday, Dov had gotten the others to resume work before the Sabbath meal, since only a few more hours of work were needed to complete the structure. They were still hammering away when Jehiel came over from the bathhouse, dressed to welcome the Sabbath. He urged them to stop; it would be sacrilegious to celebrate the holiday in a booth that had been built on the Sabbath. The others complied readily, but Dov refused. Only one short hour's work, and it would be finished! Finally — but reluctantly — he yielded to Paul's urging.

The settlers were nearly finished with their Sabbath meal when Dov came into the dining room. Paul could see at a glance that he was in a bad mood. He began to eat distractedly, then pushed his plate away. "Noah, are we raising rabbis here, or what?" he demanded.

"What do you mean?" Noah asked.

"I just went past the children's dining room. They had candles on the table and Arieh was making the benediction. Then they sang psalms!" Dov seemed outraged by all this.

"What's wrong with psalms?" Noah asked, smiling indulgently. "They're hymns of praise, or thanksgiving..."

"What's wrong!" Dov's voice rose indignantly. "Next thing you know, they'll be wanting a synagogue and ..."

"But they've been doing this for months!" Ora put in. "You just hadn't noticed."

Dov gave the table a short blow with his fist. "None of us are religious — why, then, let the children start ..."

"Why do they do it?" Noah asked. He looked thoughtfully at Dov, considering the question. "Why? Because there's a need," Noah said, answering his own question. "It has a psychological value. The children saw Jehiel doing it in his house, and it appealed to something in them. It is different from their everyday life.

"In our parent *kibbutz*," he continued, "we did away with all religious observances. On the Sabbath, we taught our children to sing socialist songs, or nature songs, and even the sentimental ones. Then a few new children came. They missed the Sabbath atmosphere they were raised in, so they read from the Bible and sang psalms. And the girls lit the Sabbath candles. Well, some of our *sabras* laughed, and some didn't. Soon, they were all doing it — even the ones who scoffed.

"And we didn't object," Noah went on, "because we saw that the children had a need for a spiritual basis to their lives. We had given them a sense of our social and national ideals and we thought that was sufficient. As you can see — it wasn't."

"But why the Bible? Why bring them up on fairy tales?" Dov's voice was antagonistic now.

Shimon, the newcomer, had stopped eating to listen. At Dov's protest, a wry smile curved across Shimon's mouth and he said, "Fairy tales? Very powerful, this fairy tale book — the source of three major religions. For over two millenniums, it has sustained our scattered people and kept them spiritually united. Heine called the Book our only Fatherland. Yes, for too many centuries it has been our portable Fatherland."

"But it teaches them to believe in God!" Dov sputtered. "From candle-lighting to psalm-singing — the next step is orthodoxy — a long step back into the middle ages!" Now Dov flared out at Noah, "Why do you encourage this? The children will no longer ask — is there a God — they'll just believe there is! Oh my God, we'll go through the whole nightmare cycle again — all those blind steps back." He swallowed hard, as if the words were stones caught in his throat.

"Nevertheless, children will always ask, 'Is there a God?'" Ora said quietly. "We want the decision to be theirs."

"Do you believe there is a God?" Dov demanded, hurling the question at her as if it were an accusation.

Ora looked at him thoughtfully. "That question will probably be the very last question the very last man on earth will ask."

"Very bright, but it doesn't answer my question."

"It's not a question that can be answered quickly," Ora said, "Oh, I answered it unhesitatingly and very positively when I was a child — I was an atheist then. Now, I am not so positive." She frowned thoughtfully and began rolling small bits of bread between her fingers.

"The skeptics say 'to see is to believe,'" Ora went on, "but we can see with more than our eyes. Moses saw God in his inner vision — and gave us the divine laws. The prophets — each saw God in his inner vision — and their truths of justice and brotherhood and love are the basis of civilization."

She frowned, as if irked with herself for expressing in such shallow words feelings that were too profound —

and elusive — for utterance. It was as if Dov had asked her to turn her soul inside out, to be gaped at and examined. Then, raising her dark eyes that had grown softly luminous, she said, "To me, this Land — it is all — well, it is all God!"

Dov was entranced for the moment by Ora's rapt look. Then he bestirred himself, sighed heavily and said, "The Jews — they're a mystery to me." He rose to go, but Paul kept him back.

"Dov, why are you building the *succoth?*"

"Because it celebrates the harvest — purely a nature festival — without religious significance!" Dov retorted.

"Every nature festival began as a tribute to some god," Paul said, grinning.

That night, Dov took his concertina into the children's quarter and soon his gay music enlivened the air. Soon, too, there was heard the piping of children's voices, hesitant at first, then lifting in a shrill chorus.

Some of the settlers grumbled. Did he have to do this on the Sabbath, when there were other nights for such singing? Was he deliberately setting the children against their parents? But others sided with Dov. There was nothing wrong with singing songs on the Sabbath Eve — orthodox Jews always welcomed it with songs. They objected not to the singing but to the kind of songs they sang, as well as Dov's reason for teaching them. Arguments broke out that were to grow bitter in the days that followed.

Ora tried to reason with Dov. "You're dividing them."

"But why? Isn't singing good for the children?" he replied.

She admitted that it was.

"Well then, what's the fuss about?"

Troubled, Ora turned to Paul. "He's dividing the settlers," she said. "Talk to him."

"But why me?" Paul asked, flattered that she had called on him for this.

"You are his friend. He admires you."

"If you can't convince him, I certainly can't," Paul said.

But, that night he spoke to Dov. "You've a grudge against religion and are working it off on the children!"

"By teaching them songs and games?" Dov snorted. When Paul looked at him skeptically, he added — in a conciliatory tone — "But it is really good for the children! You should see Erni! It's the first time he ever joined the children in songs or games — or anything else."

If a game or a few songs sung with other children could break down Erni's resistance, it would, even if in a negative sort of way, serve a good purpose, Paul thought.

When he told Ora about this, she scoffed. "Sure, Erni likes to play the games. He likes the feel of a bat in his hands. He nearly knocked out Arieh's eye with it and Arieh says it wasn't an accident. He's always up to some nastiness, the children say."

"Maybe Dov will win him over," Paul said. "He's wonderful with children."

"From your mouth to God's ear, but I doubt that it will get that far," Ora said, giving Paul one of her rare, beguiling smiles.

Gaping after her as she walked to her tent, Paul thought that miracles were still happening in the Land.

Chapter Eleven

On the Sabbath, visits were usually exchanged between the members of Tel Hashava and adjacent settlements. Since October 11th, however, when the United States delegate to the United Nations announced U.S. approval of Palestine partition, Arab violence had flared up in many villages along the eastern and northern borders. Sgt. Cassidy telephoned Noah to be on the alert for trouble. Later, he called to tell him that the raiders had been beaten off.

"In that case, it is all right for us to ride to the hill land," Ora said. "We will be back early."

"It is not all right," Noah said irritably. His eyes were bloodshot from a sleepless night, and he kept pressing his knuckles against his cheek, which was swollen. Avram had threatened to tie him up and take him to the dentist in Haifa and Noah, afraid of a session with the dentist, had finally agreed to go the day after Sabbath.

"There's no sense in taking risks," Noah said, when Ora's face took on its obstinate look. "You can go when the Agency settles the matter."

Ora pointed out that only a few *dunum* of the hill land was in dispute, that the rest was theirs to visit — if not to work. Besides, she promised to avoid the highways.

Paul, who earlier — with Avram and Dov — had agreed

to go, hoped that Noah would succeed in dissuading Ora. He had felt enormously pleased when she had invited him along. It was almost as if she had asked him for a date. But now he thought it would be a rash adventure.

With a heavy sigh, Noah yielded. He knew that once Ora's mind seized on anything, it was easier to make a river run upstream than change it.

When they were ready to go and the mules were brought out of the barn, Paul was surprised to see Avram lifting Emmi onto the back of a particularly brutish-looking mule. He thought it was reckless of them to take her.

Dov rode on Chaveh, a mule with a stubborn disposition, while Paul felt secure on Nesher (Eagle), so named because of its slow, plodding walk and docile temperament.

With Ora in the lead, the five proceeded to the north border of the *kibbutz*, passing Jehiel's *succoth* which was covered over with twists of brush and festooned with oranges, apples, eggplants, pumpkins and corn.

The clop-clop behind Paul ceased and he could hear Dov cursing. He turned. Dov shook a fist at the mule. "You four-footed Arab devil! No monkey business or I'll flay you alive!"

Sensing that the rider meant business, the animal bestirred itself into a trot. Dov chuckled. "Mules and women. The fist is the best persuader."

"Try it on Ora," Paul said.

"She's something else again," Dov grinned. "The new sex they're raising here. Part mule, part devil."

Boulder Hill and the long, even furrows of the vineyard were behind them now. The earth was pitted with holes they had dug that week. The feather-shaped leaves of the young eucalyptus trees fluttered in the wind.

Ora was riding Gittel, the beast with the unpredictable temperament, and she had let it know who was master at the outset. Gittel veered neither to the right nor the left, except at his mistress' command.

Those *sabras*, Paul reflected admiringly. They were such a positive type, so self-reliant and unfalteringly sure of themselves. They were made to feel that they were the prized ones of the land, yet they were not sheltered as his sister had been sheltered by his parents. No *sabra* could remember peaceful times. Perhaps this was what toughened them and made them so undaunted.

With Avram and Dov on either side of her, Emmi felt herself securely guarded. Once, her mule stopped short before something that was crawling by. Avram leaned over and spoke in a low, quieting voice and the beast plodded on. Emmi was enjoying the ride, but she wished that the mule's hide wasn't so rough. She felt as if a grater were rubbing against her flesh.

The land began its gentle rise and Ora led them along the spine of a hill, then across a *wadi*. The mules stepped gingerly over clusters of low, needle-sharp bushes. For long stretches, the ground was scorched by the sun. Decayed plants lay like scabs on its bald surface.

Now and then, Ora urged her mule on to a faster pace. The early morning wind whipped her hair across her face and with a quick toss, she flung it back. There was something untamed in the gesture, and Paul thought it a pity that she did not have an Arab steed — one that could outride the wind and leap across mountain peaks.

They passed a Bedouin encampment, and its black goat-skin tents looked like monstrous, landlocked bats. Overhead, a flock of crows swooped earthward and then vanished in the brush. A dog gave chase, and a few children scrambled after it. A small girl in a ragged black shift sat on the ground scratching her head. When the riders approached, she looked up and Paul could see flies on her pus-filled eyelids.

The land levelled, walled in on one side by *sangas,* massive, cave-like boulders. Then, for a long stretch, boulders faced each other across a dirt road. Everywhere, the earth was covered with rocks, as if an earthquake had splintered a mountain and spewed its fragments onto the ground.

"Our land of milk and honey," Dov remarked.

"It was — and will be again," Avram retorted.

The chaotic desolation of the land was appalling and Paul recalled someone saying that Palestine was God's first attempt at creation — from which He learned what to avoid in creating the rest of the world.

A row of markers came into view. Reaching them, Ora dismounted and tethered her mule. With a groan of relief, Paul slid to the ground, lurching as his legs folded under him. Avram swung Emmi down and she wobbled comically, like a colt trying out its legs for the first time.

"Isn't it beautiful here?" Avram cried out. Emmi limped after him. "We are on top of the world!" he went on elatedly. "We will build a *kibbutz* that will be the pride of all Palestine! Look, Emmi, let me show you!" Seizing her hand, he pulled her along over the stones.

"First, we will build the communal house, more beautiful than ours below. Then, the children's home and then little houses with gardens, for the married ones. It will be on a grand scale!"

Emmi stared at him, incredulous. Avram was either joking or utterly mad! All she could see was a dismal, rock-strewn bareness that stretched away in vast lengths to the hills. All she could feel was pain from the stones under her feet!

It was awful! A chaos, as in the beginning of creation, lying at the very edge of the world. Emmi shuddered at the prospect of living here.

Her silence subdued Avram. He thought himself a fool to be swept away by the blueprint in his mind. Emmi looked so small and delicate and her little arched nose was beginning to redden in the sun. He wanted to lift her up in his arms and carry her over the stones. But instead, he strode off to join the others.

Ora was unrolling a map she had brought and she began explaining where everything would be — the watchtower, the barn, the machine shed, the school, the dwellings.

"But water — there isn't any," Emmi said.

"You won't go thirsty, I promise you," Avram answered with a finality that removed all doubt.

Dejected, Ora rolled up the map. Apart from Avram, none had shared the excitement of these new beginnings. It had been a mistake to invite them along. They had no vision. They could see only the tangible, and their pessimism showed on their faces. She kicked at a stone, then bent to pick it up and took it over to the markers. She brought another. Then she went to work in earnest.

Watching her, Paul marvelled. She loves even this God-forsaken waste! Truly, the land was her religion. He exchanged a meaningful glance with Dov as he saw her stagger under the weight of a huge rock. Then, he, too, began picking them up.

"A land whose stones are iron," he said, grinning at Dov.

"And out of whose hills thou mayest dig brass." Dov finished the words from *Deuteronomy* and added cynically, "We should live so long."

Paul stooped to remove some pebbles that were clinging to the soles of his shoes. They felt damp as he touched them and he knelt down and fingered the earth.

It was not hard and bone dry like the rest of the ground around him but felt spongelike and clung moistly to his fingers. Ora saw him kneeling and went over to him.

"It's damp here," Paul said, as she looked questioningly at him. She dropped down beside him and began scooping up the earth with a stick. They worked silently, removing bits of rotted wood, clumps of weeds and debris. A dead frog lay sprawled out stiffly. Its legs looked like twists of rotted string. Ora shivered and, watching her, Paul grinned thinking, she's more feminine than she realizes.

"It might be a spring — or a river bed," Ora said.

Paul nodded. If this was a buried water vein, the settlers would not lack water!

Avram came over. His face kindled at the dark stain on the ground. He picked up a green clump of earth, sniffed and cried out, "Algae! There must be water here!"

"Paul found it," Ora said.

Paul felt oddly elated as Ora spoke.

Dov, who had brought their bag of provisions over to the mound of stones, set to work with Emmi collecting brushwood, to make a fire. Avram came running over.

"Stop! We can't have a fire! The smoke will be seen! No sense in letting the Arabs know we're here."

"Why not?" Dov demanded. "It's our land!"

"That's a point they're contesting," Ora said dryly. "There will be time enough to test their temper when we take possession."

The mist had lifted as they mounted their mules to return. In the glare of the sun, Paul could see the Arab village on the heights, with its blue-domed mosque and slender minaret. Black-garbed women stood around a well. The nearness of the Arabs, together with the Bedouin encampment below, gave Paul an uneasy feeling of hostile encirclement.

Through the lane of boulders, two Arabs came riding toward them, their rifles glinting in the sun. Paul saw the quick shudder that went through Emmi. He pressed his mule closer so that he could reach out to her, while Avram, who had been riding ahead, now waited, giving her a reassuring smile.

The Arabs continued at a trot, neither slowing their pace nor veering aside to let the settlers pass. But Ora rode on. Paul could feel his stomach contracting and sweat broke out on his forehead. The Arabs were wearing European jackets and white *kefiyahs,* the ends of which were drawn around the lower part of their faces.

Ora was mad! Recklessly mad — to challenge them for the right of way! She was risking their lives out of pride —not principle. If Dov or Avram didn't tell her to swerve to the side, he would!

Suddenly, as Ora advanced, the Arabs sidled to the right. Paul caught the venomous look each gave her, and their snarl of words.

Turning around, Ora called out to them in Arabic, her voice snapping out like a harsh command. The Arabs reined in their horses and Ora trotted over to them. The imperious tone of her voice and haughty lift of her head sent the look of contempt from their faces. One of the Arabs said something, and Ora replied in a staccato, whip-stinging tone.

"Yes, the girl was utterly mad, Paul thought, as he looked nervously from Avram to Dov. But neither of them seemed anxious. Instead, they were grinning!

One of the Arabs muttered something and Ora — with

a curt nod, as if dismissing them — turned her mule around. Their eyes followed her with looks of reluctant admiration.

"What happened?" Paul asked.

"They called us sons of dogs, and Ora asked why they insulted their own fathers, inasmuch as Arabs and Jews have a common father in our ancestor Abraham," Avram said.

"That Ora!" Dov chuckled. "Not part mule. All devil!"

Emmi forced a smile to her face, but it was a feeble one. Inwardly, she felt sick with fright. Her blood had chilled in that terrifying, endless moment when the Arabs came riding straight toward them. How sinister they had looked, with their rifles! It made her feel faint just to think of them.

When they moved to the hill land, they would be encircled by Arabs, Emmi brooded. And there would be trouble — the kind that Tante Emmi had never written about, but which had taken her life. Yes, life on the hill would be primitive — cruder even than at Tel Hashava. There would be nothing but work and trouble and loneliness — and sudden death.

And Alan would not come because the hill land was in another district; she would never see him again. This thought was even more shattering than the other.

After the bare, desolate hills, Tel Hashava — with its green plantings and dwellings — looked particularly inviting to Paul. Music from the radio and the shouts of children at play lifted his spirits. Groups of settlers sat on the lawn, some reading books or newspapers. Several infants lay naked on blankets, in the sun. It was all pleasantly idyllic, Paul thought, after the raw, impoverished look of the Bedouin encampment.

A car was parked in front of the office, and Paul heard Avram call out, "That's Hassan's." Ora did not reply but Paul could see her straightening her blouse and smoothing back her hair. She was excited, Paul knew, and he was irked with himself for feeling a stab of jealousy.

Erni came running over, waving his arms. "Emmi! He is here!" A sudden radiance on Emmi's face irritated Paul. And the trip to the hill losts its pleasure for him then of a shared adventure. The feeling of hoplessness that had seized Emmi vanished the moment she saw Alan.

"I'd just about given you up," he said, holding out his arms to help her down. "How was it?"

"Quite nice," she replied, wanting to cling to him when he lifted her from the back of the mule. She had the sensation of her legs being washed from under her, and she swayed.

"Steady, girl," Alan said, catching her by her arms.

"I'm not much of a rider," Emmi said. She smiled ruefully.

"That isn't much of a horse, either."

"Was he a nuisance?" Emmi asked, pointing to Erni.

"Not half bad," Alan said. Grinning down at Erni, he ruffled his hair, hoping he wouldn't say anything about how angry Alan had been when he learned Emmi had ridden to the hills.

They had no business going there, Capt. Ainslee had warned them. It wasn't theirs yet. It's a wonder the Arabs hadn't attacked them, the temper they were in these days.

And Erni's telling Alan had only made matters worse, since Alan wasn't supposed to be there. If he called Sgt. Cassidy for permission to ride after them, there'd be a terrible fuss. It would mean the end for sure, if the captain found out about his visit. The pickup had passed

Tel Hashava and Alan had dropped off there just long enough for a quick hello to Emmi. That was an hour ago, and he had been sweating it out ever since. Until then, he had had no idea that the girl had such a hold on him.

"You shouldn't have gone," Alan said to Emmi.

She smiled, wishing she hadn't. Avram took the mule into the barn and brushed roughly against Alan. He neither smiled nor apologized, and Emmi wished he wouldn't behave so badly each time Alan came.

"Was it quiet up there?" Alan asked. "I was worried."

"There was no need to worry, not really," Emmi said.

They walked toward the dwellings. Shimon was sitting on a bench next to the barn, in the shade cast by the roof's overhang. The vizor of his cap was pulled low over his bony face. Bracha came toward him with a glass of milk.

Remembering that Shimon might be here illegally, Emmi tried to detour around the barn, but Bracha had seen her.

"How was it up there?" she asked.

"Quite nice," Emmi replied. She flushed as Shimon, glancing up, saw the man in British uniform. Shimon's jaw firmed as he resumed his reading.

"Haven't seen him before," Alan remarked as they walked on. "New here, isn't he?"

"Oh no!" Emmi exclaimed.

Puzzled, Erni frowned. Emmi was lying! Shimon was a newcomer! Only the other day, Erni had heard Emmi discussing him with Paul. He was about to tell her so, when he caught her warning look.

They were approaching the children's section. Some boys were playing a bat and ball game that Dov had taught them. Yigal, Erni's roommate — a small, scrawny boy — and Jehiel stood watching. Yigal brightened when he saw Erni.

"Let's play the string game," he said, holding out a length of string. Emmi could see the look of refusal on Erni's face even before he spoke. "Play with him," she urged. "Yigal is very nice."

Erni shook his head. Just then, a woman appeared at the window and called Erni. Reluctantly, he went in. Yigal followed.

"He doesn't seem to be happy here, does he?" Alan asked.

Emmi shrugged.

"And you?"

"They are very kind to me," she said tonelessly.

"But they're not your sort, are they?"

A fugitive smile touched her face. Who were her sort? Those who, all her life, had peopled her world — only to cast her out of it? Or those who considered her one of themselves — like Avram, Dov and Ora.

"A girl like you ought not to be living this kind of life," Alan went on. "It's all right for the others — they've probably never had it any better — but you..." He stopped speaking. His tongue always raced ahead of his mind. There was no sense to his words — the girl had no choice.

"I'm grateful to be here, safe and wanted," Emmi said. She smiled gently as Avram's words, stored in her memory, returned.

"Wanted, yes — but safe? Well — I don't know. Things are shaping up to trouble. You ought to clear out."

"But where could I go? I don't know anyone else besides you and the settlers."

"You could find a job easily, an educated girl like you. There are not many like you here, I can tell you. Yes

— you ought to get work in Haifa . . ."

Emmi gaped blankly at Alan, as if he had said something so far beyond the bounds of the possible that she could not cope with it. Then, in that same instant of incredulity, she thought — why is this impossible? Had she not earned her tuition by assisting her music master with his beginning students?

The thought excited her, and she cried, "I can teach piano! I studied for many years. And I can teach German, also. I will make myself useful!" She seized Alan's arm excitedly.

The pleading look on Emmi's face stirred him and he wanted to take her in his arms and promise to protect and provide for her. But the censor in his mind reached out to restrain him.

"Let's think about it, shall we?" he said gently. "I'm due for a holiday, I'll ask around . . ."

Emmi's hand dropped from his arm and he could see the hope draining from her. He felt a twinge of guilt, as if he had beguiled her with a false promise.

"Now let's not get discouraged before we even try! Mind, I'm not promising I can do anything, but I'll do my best. But you must be sure you want to leave . . ."

"Oh yes, I am certain! And Erni — oh, he will . . ."

"I wouldn't say anything, not yet. Now you forget we spoke about it. There's a good girl. I ought to be waiting at the gate. The pickup should be back now . . ."

The pickup had just pulled up outside the gate when they reached it. The pensive smile on Emmi's face made Alan say, with more cheeriness than he felt, "Maybe I'll have good news next time I come. Cheer up — that's a good girl." Tipping her chin with his knuckles, he coaxed a smile to her uplifted face.

"When will you come again?" Emmi asked.

"We're not allowed social visits — but I'll come. Soon as I can make it," he said, as he hopped onto the truck.

Slowly, Emmi walked back to the dwellings. Alan must think her a child to seize on so fragile a reed as hope. She must not delude herself with thoughts of teaching. Nothing so good could happen to her.

A book on Shimon's lap lay closed. He was quoting Heine from memory and the lyrical flow of his voice held Emmi's attention. Her father had read to her and Erni this way during the long nights of waiting. She sat down beside Shimon and he took her hand and tucked it inside his. After awhile, unknowingly, Emmi leaned her head against his shoulder.

Shimon's voice flowed on as he read the familiar words. For Emmi, there were thoughts of home in the reading and the sweet, sad contentment of things remembered and loved.

Noah was climbing out of Hassan's car when Ora arrived. One side of his mouth was stiff and a thread of dried blood stained his cheek. His face twisted sideways when he tried to smile.

"Hassan flew like the devil was after us!" Noah said. To Hadar haCarmel and back — all in three hours!" Clucking at the wonder of it, he left.

"What happened?" Ora asked.

"With time out for the tooth-pulling!" Hassan called after Noah. "And don't forget, I won the wager!"

Ora pulled at Hassan's sleeve and repeated her question.

"He wouldn't go to the dentist until you returned," Hassan replied. "I wagered we would go and be back before you returned. He's even worse than we were when he used to take us to have our teeth filled. Remember?" he said, smiling.

"Yes," Ora said, smiling back. She wished that she had gone to her tent to change her clothes. She felt self-conscious that the smell of mule and of her own sweat was heavy on her.

Hassan patted the seat in his car. "I haven't much petrol . . ."

"Oh — no more riding!" Ora said. "I want to be on my feet!" she added, laughing. Hassan got out of the car.

Couples were strolling along the road, while small groups of people sat on benches outside the concrete building, talking excitedly. Dvora sat huddled over a book — Shimon's influence, Ora knew. The "anti-intellectual" had even attended his lecture!

"I'm surprised they're not walking all over the hill," Hassan remarked as he and Ora began climbing it. Ora smiled wryly. The shots that had killed Aunt Emmi had come from the opposite ridge. Only Dov and she ventured here, these days.

Neither spoke as the ascent became steeper and rougher. They paused before they reached the summit, caught by the awesome beauty of the view. Tawny waves rose fold upon fold in the distance, merging with the craggy heights of Gilboa.

Hassan slipped his arm about Ora's shoulder as they stood together letting the peace and serenity of the scene enfold them.

It was to dream a moment like this, that Ora would come here. Strangely, the reality seemed less real than the dream. There was something lacking — something disquieting — that diminished the reality.

Hassan turned to face Ora and touched her lips lightly

at first, with his. Then his arms tightened about her and he kissed her throat.

"Let me go!" she cried hoarsely, struggling out of his embrace. Shaken, she walked away from him. It was the first time he had kissed her so passionately and while it roused excitement in her, it also touched off a feeling of resentment. It was not just time and distance that had separated them — Hassan had too much to account for before Ora could feel the old oneness of their belonging together.

"What is it, Ora?" he asked, sitting down beside her on the ground, his hands cupping her shoulders.

She turned to face him, looking at the handsome cut of his white linen suit, his sleek black hair, glistening with pomade, the vermilion polish of his nails. She smiled cryptically.

"Before, I used to know what you were thinking even before you spoke. But not anymore. Not since — since you've grown so elegant."

Hassan drew back with a look of pained surprise and of anger. He said, "What's come over you, Ora? You've become so capricious. You had no trouble reading my mind when I was here before . . ."

"Two weeks ago!" she broke in. "That's a long absence for one so in love. What makes you think you can come back into my life whenever it is convenient — or safe . . ."

"Safe? What do you mean, safe?"

"You know what I mean! Two months ago, we were attacked. Three wounded, two dead. Dr. Emmi, remember her? She got you well each time you were sick. You must have read about it — all the papers printed it — only the Arab press made a victory of it. Why didn't you come? Are your British friends so intriguing that you couldn't spare us even a moment of consolation? Yes — you've returned a different person. Oh, so polished, so very elegant!"

"How could I come, when I was in England?"

"Your semester had already ended!"

"I stayed on for student conferences. I knew nothing of the attack! Nothing! But you haven't changed — you are still all lightning and thunder!"

Why had she lashed out at him? She had not even thought to speak of this when suddenly, inexplicably, the bitterness of doubt, of suspicion, erupted. Doubt and suspicion — the poison they now breathed in with the air. She said reproachfully, "Why didn't you answer my letters?"

"But I did! I answered every letter at once!"

"With nothings," she snapped back. "You never answered about what happened to our friends at the university. Why didn't they speak up?"

"But they did speak up — or don't you listen to the radio? They've followed Tewfik..."

"Tewfik!" Ora spat out the name as if it were an obscenity. Then she lapsed into silence, her eyes filled with a dark brooding. Tonelessly, she said, "Tewfik — I used to think him a god among men. What made him change, Hassan?"

"We all change. The reality of things as they are — not as we dream them — gives us a new perspective..."

"Words, Hassan, just words. The reality is that the Jews have brought capital into the land — and science — and progress. As a result, Palestine Arabs have the highest standard of living of all Arab countries. Tewfik himself said this only three years ago, remember? It is even more true now."

Hassan nodded gloomily. He had hoped to push the moment of reckoning into the future — but Ora was always ready to pin one down to the immediacy of things.

When she resumed speaking, her voice was soft, with a wistful calm to it. "Only three years ago, Tewfik said, 'they are coming back — our brothers in Abraham — they are returning from exile with skills and learning, and we will be a country of two brother-nations living as one. *Echud* — unity!' Remember, Hassan, when he said this?"

Nodding, Hassan wondered at the mildness of her tone. It was as though summoning up the quality she had loved most in their friend and leader had quieted her.

". . . and he used to be so mild, to have such self-control in everything he did or said. Now, he sounds as if he is choking with anger. He rants over the radio just as that madman did, in Berlin. If only I knew why he changed."

"Would that change anything — knowing?" Hassan asked.

Ora was silent a moment, then a sudden excitement kindled her eyes. "Hassan, arrange for me to see him!" she cried, seizing his hand.

"You are mad! Four of our old *Echud* group died — for talking unity! Tewfik has no wish to become a martyr!"

"You don't even want to try!" Ora said. She flung his hand from her. "Are you afraid to talk unity? Where do you stand? How do you feel, about — about what we used to believe in?"

Her question was the sick core in him, unanswered these many months because resolving it required either more courage or less conscience than was in him.

Finally, he said, "The end of British colonial rule . . ."

"The British will cease ruling us by next August," she broke in, with a wave of her hand. "But what after that?"

Hassan lowered his head as if her probing eyes bared more than he dared reveal even to himself. "But does it matter, what I want? Is it up to you or me to settle these questions?"

"It matters to me — I must know!" she flared up again. "We can help the situation! Another start to *echud* must be made. And quickly, before the Mandate ends. Surely, not all of our comrades have rejected unity . . ."

Suddenly, anger welled up in Hassan. Ora spoke as if the Arabs had caused all the trouble — as if the Zionists were innocent of wrongdoing! "Your people work hard to make Zionism acceptable to the west. If only they made the same effort with us!"

Ora's silence and the droop of her head were like an acquiescence. Hassan reached for her hand. "Ora, don't turn from me." Gently, he touched her face, turning it toward him. "Don't let our people's troubles divide us, Ora. We are one."

She turned then, and was in his arms.

Chapter Twelve

A greyness set in, with the first few days of October. Daily, the sky was overcast, and the raw bite of an early winter was in the air. The weather, Noah assured Emmi, was misbehaving; it was most unseasonable. But this was small comfort to the ten-tdwellers who remembered the storms of the previous winter and did not relish the prospect of others, under roofs that drenched them.

Strangely, Emmi did not find tent living unpleasant. She enjoyed the coziness, when the lamp was lit. The light threw shadows like moving pictures on the canvas walls and an earthy smell of growing things seeped through. And Ora, these past few days, had been in a happy mood. She was so friendly, in fact, that Emmi could not get over the change in her. It must be as the girls in the laundry said — Ora was in love with that handsome Arab!

It was pleasant, too, to hear the voices from the nearby tents. Dov and Paul never stopped a discussion until the others shouted to them for silence. Then amusing — or sarcastic — comments would fly back and forth in Hebrew or English, and Ora and Emmi would burst into laughter.

Sometimes, Emmi would lie awake listening to the

singing. Dov was proud of his chorus, and with good reason. He was an exacting conductor and made the singers keep repeating phrases until they achieved the tonal effect he wanted. They enlivened the nights with their gay Russian or Yiddish songs, but Emmi loved best the plaintive pioneer songs they sang so feelingly.

She could distinguish voices, now. Bracha, for all her great bulk, had a light, sweet voice. Ora's was deeper — a contralto, with high notes that rang true and firm. Shlomo's tenor quivered on the high notes, but his middle register was wonderfully sweet. Emmi could hardly associate that beautiful voice with Shlomo's monkeylike face.

But best of all, and most comforting, was Shimon's nearness in the tent opposite hers. The cone of light from his open tent was like the hall light back home. There, Emmi would fall asleep with its golden streak shimmering at the edge of the door. Later, her father would tiptoe into her room to see that all was well. When he closed the door, the streak of light would no longer be there, but knowing her father was home, Emmi would drift off to sleep again, comforted.

Yes, it was very reassuring, this feeling she had about Shimon. There was a sense of her father's presence whenever he was near. But Emmi never ventured a remark to him unless he paused to invite one. Awe at his renown and her shyness combined to make her acutely aware of her own insignificance. And there was that nagging question that still remained unanswered — had he been on the same ship with her mother? But she knew she could not ask him. Illegal immigrants, when caught by the British, were returned to the point from which they had fled. — Or worse. The settlers had absorbed

Shimon as if he had been there from the start and this was his protection.

Because of a leg injury, he had been given office work and the job of tending the vegetable garden. From the storehouse, Emmi could see his gaunt figure plucking up weeds, the bony hands gently rooting a plant. Shimon took pleasure in this work, she knew. His face had the same contented look her father's had, when he tended the garden.

For all the comfort she felt from his presence, though, it was Shimon who touched off fears in her that made her seize on Alan's promise. It happened on a Sabbath Eve. Emmi saw Shimon sitting, with others, around a candlelit table in Jehiel's hut. He was wearing a skull-cap, and the bright little flames from the candle mellowed the sharp boniness of his face. It was his expression, the look of ecstasy on his face, that intrigued Emmi — as though songs long pent up had suddenly found a glorious release.

Later, when Shimon returned to his tent, he called out *Shabbat shalom* to Emmi. She told him of how she had listened to the singing.

"But, why did you not come in, child?" he asked.

"I — I was not invited."

"Do you need an invitation, to sing to God? We sang *zemiroth*, table hymns in tribute to Queen Sabbath. Did your parents not observe the Sabbath?"

"Once, when I was very little, Tante Emmi took me to a synagogue in Berlin ..." Emmi shrugged off the rest.

Shimon's cracked, leathery lips twisted in a half smile. "We Jews were German even with our God," he said. "I don't wonder you were not drawn into going to services again. Our services were correct — but impersonal. Respectful — and cold. Nothing intimate and spontaneously joyous like those of the Eastern Jews we used to mock. You come to Jehiel's next *Shabbat*. You will be welcome."

As Shimon turned to his tent, Emmi asked hesitantly. "What did you mean when you said this was Noah's Ark?"

"It saved us from the deluge. When we cried out for rescue, a deafness fell on all the world. But would the world have been silent if six million Christians had been slaughtered? It was a miracle that we survived Hitler. Yes, my child, be thankful for Noah's Ark."

Later, Emmi thought about what Shimon had said, and she was afraid again. It was a miracle that they had survived, he had said, but it would be an even greater miracle if the Arabs let them live.

That week, Avram called out to Emmi from his truck and handed her a package.

"For me?" she asked, incredulous. "What is it?"

"If you don't open it, you won't know," he said crossly and drove off. He had just returned from Haifa. Emmi saw him park the truck in front of one of the sheds. Lately, Avram's attitude had baffled her. Either he was friendly, as he had been several weeks ago when he had taken her to the hill land with the others, or else he ignored her completely. She did not know how to fathom his moods and dismissed as absurd the idea that he might be jealous of Alan. There is no jealousy where there is no love, and Avram, she felt certain, liked her no more than any of the other girls.

Unwrapping the package, Emmi caught her breath sharply. It was an album of music! Bach! Beethoven! Chopin! And best of all — her beloved Schumann! Clutching the precious gift with both arms, she ran over to the shed, where Avram was lifting a sack onto his shoulder.

"Avram!" she cried. "Oh, Avram . . !" But words failed her and she stared at him, speechless with emotion. Then she kissed him on his cheek and ran back to the store-house.

Smiling, Avram stroked the cheek she had kissed.

The dining room was empty when Emmi ran in. She pulled a bench over to the piano and sat down to play. She needed only to glimpse at the first bar of the Chopin prelude and the music, pent up in her memory, flowed through her fingers. A shiver went through her at the sound of the first, mournful chord. Then a strangled sob escaped her as, painfully, she remembered the past. She dropped her face into her hands and wept.

Someone began turning the pages of the music. It was Shimon. "Please play this for me," he said.

Emmi began to play and soon as if they had an independent life, her fingers glided knowingly over the keys. She could feel her sorrow for the past leaving her. Caught up in her playing, she was unaware that Bracha, rooted at the kitchen door, was listening with wonder to her playing. Or that Noah had slipped into the room. Or that the settlers, returning from the fields, were listening raptly.

It was not until later, when she began to stumble over an intricate passage, that Shimon said, "You are tired. Thank you." Glancing up, she could see Avram's eyes fixed on her, in awe. Then she saw the others. Their clapping broke the silence, and Emmi crimsoned with delight.

"What a treasure we have!" Bracha exclaimed, hugging her. Dov shook his head in disbelief. "And *I* offered to teach her music!"

The impromptu concert had an extraordinary effect on Dov. He went around with a preoccupied look and was so completely absorbed in his own thoughts that whatever he did had to be undone over again. Thousands of slips were being planted in the vineyard. Ora covered each one lightly with earth. But Dov, distracted by his thoughts, heaped enough soil over them to bury them. And in fetching water in barrels, he took it to fields where it was not needed, while Ora and the other vineyard workers stood waiting for him.

He had a problem — that was certain. The question was how to solve it. Then, suddenly, it crystallized. He was going to organize the first choral and concert ensemble in a Palestine *kibbutz!*

Some of the settlements were distinguished for their writers or artists. Tel Hashava, the farthest outpost at the eastern border, would become the music settlement!

There was musical talent here, and it was being wasted on the wilderness. Dov's chorus would consist of settlers from as many nationalities as there were countries in Europe. The "remnant of the return" had brought to their ancient homeland gifts of varied cultures from the lands of their exile, and Dov would weave all this into a harmonic synthesis!

Plunging from thought into action, he tacked a notice on the bulletin board in the dining hall requesting the members of the chorus, as well as anyone else interested in music, to attend a meeting after the evening meal.

The tables had not yet been cleared when the settlers gathered around Dov. Ora sat beside him. Accustomed to a Dov who took either a facetious or cynical view of life, they now saw one who looked grim with purpose. Ora's presence indicated that something more serious was afoot than just another of his whims.

They were going to make profitable use of the music talent in the *kibbutz*, Dov explained. They would practice and rehearse until they were judged ready for a public appearance, after which they would go on a concert tour. This, of course, would be done in the winter months, when they were not needed on the farm.

"With our earnings, we will buy tractors, farm equipment, building materials. Of course, we have much hard work ahead of us, before we are ready, but knowing our chorus and listening to Emmi at the piano, can you doubt our success?"

As Dov anticipated, those gathered here were wildly enthusiastic. But the other settlers did not hesitate to voice their opinions. Dvora was the first.

"And who will manage the kitchen when Bracha goes off? You'll all go wandering off like gypsies while, here, we'll sicken with overwork and bad food..."

Another protested that the absence of specialists, who had been trained at their expense, would cripple the work. This was a very serious complaint, and the voices grew harsh with protests.

"... and what are you, musicians or farmers?" Dvora demanded. "If musicians, why did you come here? And if farmers — why leave?"

"Listen to her — the cow on two legs!" Shlomo jeered. Others retorted and an argument broke out. Dov shouted for silence.

Emmi could not understand all that was being said, but the scowls and the heated snap of words appalled her. The wonderful project was doomed! Before she was aware of what she was doing, she cried out, "Oh, please do not quarrel! It is a wonderful idea! Music is — music is what is best in life! You don't know what it has meant to me — listening to your singing. You will make people happy..."

The passion with which she spoke amazed the settlers.

Was this the Emmi who was as mute as a shadow at meetings? Avram gaped as if another person had slipped into her skin — a girl of fire and conviction. He resented the project, but now he felt that he would clobber anyone who spoke against it.

Ora said, "Emmi, I agree with you. I'm all for it!"

Dvora screwed up her face in a look that left no doubt as to her thought. Ora — the smartest of the lot — the prized one — had taken leave of her senses!

"Don't worry, Dvora, I haven't gone crazy," Ora said laughingly. "But I don't agree that we must be either one or the other. Many settlements combine farming with other occupations. Some settlers go elsewhere to work during the winter months and turn their wages over to their *kibbutz*, as Dov proposes. And some send their most talented abroad to study art or music or science. Now *that* is a *real* sacrifice. Dov's idea is for us to express ourselves as musicians as well as farmers . . ."

Ora's words mollified a few, but failed to impress Dvora. She left in disgust.

"We need an organizer," Ora went on. "We ought to learn from the Americans — they know how to organize everything . . ."

All eyes fixed on Paul, who had come in earlier to ask Emmi — in charge of the store — for a new lamp glass since his had broken.

"But we *have* an American!" Shlomo announced gleefully.

"Not me!" Paul protested. "I have no talent for organizing anything — not even my own work. You have a great idea — all you need is practice — a lot of it — " With that, he hurried out.

When the meeting finally broke up, Emmi felt so happy and exhilarated that she was reluctant to leave. Outside, she stumbled over the step of the porch. Avram caught her.

"I feel drunk!" she giggled.

"Aren't we all?" Avram said. "And mad!" he added, with an undertone of bitterness. He had the feeling that none of this would have come about had he not bought that book of music for Emmi. She would leave Tel Hashava — she would be such a success that she would be lost to him forever.

A strong wind had risen. Then a few drops of rain fell — cold and piercing as needles. At first, the girls squealed with delight, lifting their faces to the rain. But when it suddenly came pouring down, they scrambled wildly indoors.

"I am so excited I won't be able to sleep" Emmi confessed, as Ora began fastening the flap of the tent.

"You'd better," Ora said. "In three hours, we're all going to work in the vineyard to finish planting the slips. You, too. All hands will be needed," Ora said lightheartedly.

But Emmi felt too keyed up to sleep. She thought of all that had happened in the few days since Avram had brought the music — how the settlers had praised her, and how happy their admiration had made her.

The concert, at first, seemed utterly improbable. But now, it was actually going to happen! Ora was for it, and Ora's will usually prevailed. Yes, Emmi would have a concert career after all — just as Herr Professor Mahler had predicted! She fell asleep, happy at the thought.

She woke with a scream. Something heavy and wet had fallen on her, smothering her. She cried out in fright, but the rough wet cloth muffled the sound of her screams. She struggled to free herself when suddenly, the cloth was pulled away. But her legs were tangled in rope.

"Don't move, Emmi, you'll only tangle it worse," Ora said, working at the rope. "The wind's blown down the tent."

Rain kept stinging them, driving sharp needles into their faces. People ran past, kicking up showers of mud. At last, Ora loosened the rope and the two girls fled to the dining hall. Inside, it was dark and smelled of damp, huddled bodies. Somebody grumbled.

"Don't complain!" Dov called out. "We won't have to water the fields tomorrow!"

In the darkness, a girl sat down on someone and the two giggled hysterically. People kept colliding with each other as they ran in, stumbling over those sitting on the floor. As candles in saucers were brought out of the kitchen, their flickering lights tore small orange patches from the darkness.

Wrapped in a blanket, Bracha hurried in. She stopped before Emmi, who sat shivering with cold. "You will have tea in a moment, Emmi dear," Bracha said, and with a reassuring pat, she went into the kitchen.

Emmi's wet nightgown clung to her skin. Paul and Dov offered to share their blankets with her and she blushed hotly. Then Noah appeared. Rosy with excitement, he chuckled as if nothing had really happened of consequence. He popped up everywhere, giving a comforting word here, teasing there, and scolding some for their grumbling at nature's little prank.

Something rough and dry fell on Emmi's shoulder, and she shivered. It was a blanket Avram was wrapping around her. He was wearing only his shorts and when he leaned over her, his wet, naked arms chilled her. But the gesture touched Emmi. There were many girls in the room, and he had sought her out! Everyone seemed so concerned for her, so warmly sincere, she thought.

She was startled out of her reflections by a burst of cheering. Bracha and a few girls were bringing tea and sandwiches to the table. Dov plied Emmi with food, heaping a plate for her.

"Eat, Emmi! Put some flesh on your bones or people will think a skeleton is playing tricks on the piano," he said, in German.

"Eat, Emmi, eat!" The others took up the cry and Emmi, who was famished, nearly choked with laughter.

The rain kept up a rhythmic drumming on the roof and windows as the heat from the kitchen stoves drove the chill from the air. In the soft candlelight, the settlers' faces had a rosy, bright-eyed look, like that of children relishing an escapade.

Emmi chewed contentedly at her food.

The settlers awoke to a morning that glittered with sunlight. The sky was cloudless, a bright, electric blue. It was difficult to believe that there had been a storm.

Those settlers who lived in wooden huts and had slept through the night were shocked to see the wrecked tents. At breakfast, they grumbled about the new concrete barn they were building for the livestock while their *chaverim* lived in tents, exposed to the capricious elements.

"They're right!" Shlomo said to Ora. His freckled face was puffy from lack of sleep and his red hair was still wet with rain. Then, irritably, and to no one in particular, he demanded, "Aren't we as good as cows?"

"Of course you are," Ora said amiably. "But you haven't been giving us any milk lately!"

After breakfast, Avram left to get tents from the parent *kibbutz* since several of those that were wrecked were beyond repair. Ora marvelled at the good spirits with which everyone went to the fields to work although they had slept only a few hours on the dining room benches.

The drenched earth yielded readily to the plow. With Paul at the tractor, more furrows were drawn, more holes dug and more slips were planted than on any other previous day. By three o'clock, all the land allotted to that field was under cultivation. Ora declared a semi-holiday.

When Ora returned to the settlement, she saw Hassan's car outside the office. She thought of changing her clothes, but Noah's voice stopped her. He was speaking reproachfully to Hassan! She entered the office and immediately sensed tension between them. Noah's good-bye when he went out was pleasant enough, but it rang hollow in her ears.

"What happened?" she asked Hassan anxiously.

Just then, Avram poked his head in the door and, with a look that held more defiance than elation, called out, "We've got the hill land! It's clear — we're going up tomorrow!"

Ora was at the door in a flash, her voice high with excitement. "Have we really? Is this definite?"

"All clear and ours to settle!" He walked away, whistling the gay song of the Galilee.

Ora seized Hassan's arm. "We'll be a united *kibbutz* at last!" She stopped speaking when she saw the scowl on his face.

"Come," he said, walking out.

"What is it, Hassan?" she asked worriedly as she followed him to his car. "Did you quarrel with Noah? What's wrong?"

They got into the car and he wheeled it about in a swift, jerky turn that made Ora lunge against the window. "Sorry," he said, pulling her back.

"Answer me, Hassan!" she insisted.

"We didn't quarrel," he snapped irritably.

He raced the car over the pebbled road and turned it sharply onto the paved highway, driving north into the Galilee hills. They drove past long stretches of Crown-owned land, vast wastelands overgrown with weeds, nettle, burdock and cactus bushes. Miles of unused land that separated Tel Hashava from its hill section, Ora reflected bitterly. And her people so desperately in need of living space!

If was as if Hassan had read her thoughts, for he said, "Why didn't you buy this land instead of the hill?"

"Crown land. The Agency offered everything but our souls! And we'd have thrown those in, too, if we could have bought it."

"They should have sent you to buy," he said, smiling at last. "Anybody who resists you just isn't human!"

Ora reached for his hand and gripped it hard.

The road climbed and twisted between giant *sangas*. Hassan wheeled the car onto its soft shoulder and parked. His dark, lean face had a strained look. Then, with a deep sigh, he took Ora in his arms. "Ora, let's go off together. There's no other way for us." He kissed her eyelids.

A long moment passed before the meaning of his words reached her. She drew away from him and looked at him as an indulgent mother might, whose child had spoken foolishly. She smoothed back a lock of hair from his forehead and said, "You ought not to talk such nonsense, dearest."

"But I am serious!" he said.

"Leave this country? As if you or I could live anywhere else!"

"But we can have no life here together. Things won't improve. Believe me — they'll get worse . . ."

"Why worsen? Look at all we're doing to improve conditions."

"For yourselves, yes, but . . ."

"What do you mean — for ourselves!" She pulled away from him angrily. "There isn't an Arab village that hasn't benefited from the Jewish settlements. We cleared malarial swamps — Arabs are in better health, as a result. We pay the largest part of the education budget although we're a minority . . ."

"Stop sounding like a Zionist rally!" Hassan said. "I'm only telling you how Arabs feel about all the land you're buying . . ."

"We're not buying — we're ransoming the land . . ."

"And dispossessing the *fellaheen*. They won't have it — they're determined to be master in their own house . . ."

Ora gaped as if a mask had suddenly dropped from Hassan's face, revealing a hostile stranger. "But you never spoke this way before — it sounds like Arab supremacy! Why — it's no better than Nazi supremacy!"

"Would you like it to be Jewish supremacy?" Hassan asked.

"But why must there be supremacy at all?"

"Because — it is in the nature of things," Hassan replied.

"But — what became of our plans for a Jewish-Arab bi-national state . . ." Suddenly, Ora stopped as despair choked back her words. There was an enemy inside her lover, and she was sick with fear that the enemy would take control and set him against her.

Hassan shook his head wearily. "That is exactly what I mean, Ora. There can be no peace for our love here. If you love me, you will come away with me. We can live in England. Any country will be home to us as long as we are together."

A stabbing pain went through Ora. The land had never contended as a rival for Hassan's love before. Their feeling for the land was inextricably woven into their lives. It was as basic to them as their blood and bones. How could they live elsewhere? Their love would be a mutual reproach to them if they went into exile.

Ora leaned her head on Hassan's shoulder to delay her reply. He stroked her hair. "I can't go back to Oxford and leave you here, Ora. I'd worry..."

"You needn't go back to England you could return to the Hebrew University..." Instantly, she regretted what she had said. None of their Arab classmates were there, she knew.

They were silent for awhile, then Hassan said, "Ora, don't let them go up to the hill. Be patient..."

Ora sat upright. "Hassan, we are not guests in the Land! We need no invitation to go into our house!"

"Then Tewfik was right," Hassan said bitterly.

"What do you mean?"

"He said there was no sense in his seeing you. That, like the others, you would speak sincerely — and act treacherously..."

Ora gasped in outrage. "Tewfik said that?"

"He said that soon Galilee will be all Arab. You must convince Noah that it would be madness to go to the hill land now."

Had they sent Hassan with a warning? Ora wondered. She studied him a long moment and then said quietly, "Just the same, we will go up."

"No compromise is possible with fanatics!" Hassan exclaimed, his teeth clenched.

"You should know," Ora replied, "coming from a nation of fanatics."

Dusk had deepened into night by the time Ora returned to the settlement. The *kibbutz* had melted into

the darkness but oblongs of light from the concrete building shimmered on the ground. She could see the crowd
in the dining hall and hear their jubilant singing as
they stomped their feet in a *hora*. She should be rejoicing with them, but somehow she could feel no joy in
this celebration.

The new tent stood in the same spot as the other one.
With her flashlight, Ora could see that Emmi had arranged everything. The cots were neatly made up, with
the chest of drawers between them. Emmi's trunk, covered with her paisley shawl, stood up-ended.

Ora lay down on her cot and stared into the darkness.
Hassan's face appeared before her, as stony-faced as in
his farewell at the gate. What had gone wrong with him?

If love was the desire and the need one had for another, then surely his impassioned kisses, his urging to
go away with him was proof of his love. But why go
elsewhere, to fulfill this love? Who demanded this sacrifice of them?

Did Hassan want her to go off with him because, married to a Zionist, he would be considered a traitor to the
Arab cause? Ora dismissed this idea at once. Hassan was
never more fearless than when he was confronted by
danger or challenge.

What, then, had made him talk as he did?

A voice outside the tent startled her. "Ora — are you
all right?" It was Avram.

"Of course I'm all right!" she snapped.

"We're celebrating the hill land — why aren't you
there?"

"I'll be along soon. You go back. No, wait — I'll come
with you now." She straightened her blouse, ran a comb
through her hair and left the tent. Silently, she and Av-

ram walked the length of the pebbled road that led to the concrete building.

"Did Hassan say anything?" Avram asked warily. He could see that Ora was in a bad mood. She must have quarrelled with Hassan, for his car had dropped her off at the gate of the settlement.

"Nothing that we don't already know," she answered. "But don't you put him in the camp of the enemy!" she cried out savagely.

"Then he ought not to speak like one," Avram said evenly.

Tables had been pushed against the walls, and the settlers were crowded around Noah. He was singing, reading the words of the song from a paper that he held at arm's length and beating time for himself with his other hand.

Ora listened. He must have just written the song — he was always writing songs for other settlements. He had no gifts for poetry or music really, but he always managed to give meaning to his words, and to set them to a simple tune.

Noah took his song seriously and now and then, as he stressed a word, his head would jerk and his plume of white hair would nod an accent for him.

"In Tel Hashava, in Tel Hashava,
   We plow and we sow like our people of old,
   We pulled up the roots that lay dead in the earth
   And planted our own to give us new birth.

"In Tel Hashava, in Tel Hashava,
   We're building a life in our old Homeland,
   In freedom and brotherhood our children we'll rear,
   To live as Jews without shame or fear."

There was a wild burst of applause when he finished. He was pleased, and a childish grin appeared on his face.

"A song of our own! Wonderful!" Dov clapped him on the back.

"Sing it again, Noah!" Bracha urged, and the others took up the cry. Dov struck a few chords on his concertina while, at the piano, Emmi rippled the melody across the keys. More voices took up the song now, as others clapped out the rhythm with their hands.

Everyone seized on the song as if it were a banner in their hands and then, because Noah had given them still one more thing to celebrate, the settlers leaped to their feet and, linking their arms, danced around him. The air stormed with their voices.

Dov seized Ora and swung her into the round dance, and Paul hooked an arm around her shoulder. She felt no song inside her until they sang, "Who will build the Galilee?"

Then she shouted the answer like a challenge. *"We will build the Galilee!"*

PART THREE

Chapter Thirteen

The sun had not yet risen but already the set-tlers were bustling with activity. No one need-ed prodding; the spur that roused them was the hill land. This morning, they were to take posses-sion. A sense of excitement, subdued but pervasive, was in the air.

Approaching the dining hall, Paul saw three trucks. He looked inquiringly at Dov, who said, "They're from our parent *kibbutz*. Volunteers, who'll give us a hand up there."

The dining room was as crowded as on the Sabbath, when the Haifa members came. For the occasion, Bracha had covered the trestle tables with white cloths. Up front, where the volunteers were sitting, an old man was mak-ing a speech. Wearing a high-necked Tolstoyan shirt and corduroy trousers, he stood tall and barrel-chested, his coarse features dignified by a luxurious mass of white hair. In a basso voice that vibrated throughout the room like a deep-toned cello, he spoke of the traditions the settlers had inherited and of the significance of the work they were undertaking.

The settlers sat immobile, listening intensely. The speak-er was flanked by four youths wearing the tunics and military hats of the auxiliary police. Paul and Dov found places next to several husky young men who ate without once looking up at the speaker. When the orator finished and the applause broke out, the young men exchanged smiles that were at once indulgent and sarcastic.

"They're the *Palmach* boys," Dov whispered. "Nothing to worry about when they're around."

Paul was surprised at their youthfulness — some were barely out of their teens! They were a hardy-looking lot, "toughs" with ideals. *Palmach* — the "shock unit" of the *Haganah*.

Ora and Emmi were sitting at a nearby table, their caps pulled low over their foreheads. They were wearing khaki work shirts and denim trousers. It was sheer lunacy to let Emmi come along, Paul thought.

When the meal ended, the pioneers were herded into trucks. An auxiliary Hebrew policeman rode in each cab, next to the driver. The settlers remaining behind called out their good wishes and waved as the convoy began moving. Bracha came running out with heavy baskets in her hands and the settlers, teasing, warned her not to fall in love with the two *Haganah* youths who were helping her climb onto the truck.

"It is fun, going off like this!" Emmi remarked.

Avram nodded glumly as he hopped onto the cab of his truck. He was angry because Noah had yielded to Emmi's plea to be allowed to go. In her rough work clothes and cap pulled low, she looked absurdly childish. The *Haganah* boys, sitting opposite, grinned at her.

For awhile, they rode in silence. Emmi's mind went back over all that had happened in the past few days. It still seemed so unreal, and yet it satisfied her deepest longings. Oh, but she would exert herself to the point of exhaustion to prove worthy of their confidence in her. She would practice until her fingers ached. She touched Dov's

shoulder with her cheek and looked up at him, excited
at her thoughts of the future. He flicked an imaginary
fly from her nose.

The smooth band of the concrete road thrust its way
between fields of scorched weeds. Several Arab women,
their dusty gowns billowing in the wind, squeezed at
clumps of earth until drops of water oozed into their
petrol cans. They paused to stare at the convoy, then, cans
lifted to their heads, moved gracefully toward the huddle
of black, goat-skin tents that was the Bedouin encampment.

Leaving the paved highway, the convoy now joggled
over stony, untracked fields. Slowly, it climbed to the
hill land. Markers were now visible and the trucks drew
up before them. By the time Avram had parked, Noah
was already striding across the field, chart in hand, assigning tasks. Paul noticed that while the settlers and the
volunteers from the Parent *kibbutz* gathered around Noah,
the auxiliary police and *Haganah* youths fanned out in
all directions toward the outer fields. And by the time he
reached Noah, they were nowhere to be seen. Paul, Dov
and Avram were assigned to dig the well.

Dov set to work with a zeal that sent the clods of earth
flying in all directions. Avram's pace was slower, stead-
ier. And Paul's matched it.

Before long, Dov paused to wipe the sweat that was
streaming down his face. "Sweat — that's the only water
we'll find here," he said.

"The wilderness and the parched Land shall be glad,

"I will make the dry land springs of water," Avram
quoted.

Paul grinned. The uses of the Bible! It was a guide for
the hydraulic engineers for it spelled out the water veins

of ancient cities; it was history and it was law — and it contained the most dramatic narratives of saints and sinners in all literature.

Emmi came over with a pail of water. Sweat trickled down her face from under her cap, and the bridge of her nose was a fiery red. Her trousers clung wetly to her ankles. Avram frowned, pointing to them.

"I — I didn't see the swamp," she stammered.

"Any mosquito bites?" he asked. He examined her arms. She crimsoned then, as he rolled up her trouser legs. "Several bites right here. You'd better have them treated," he said. "Come along."

How gallant! Paul thought sarcastically, as he watched Avram hurrying Emmi to the first-aid truck. But he noticed that Emmi was still carrying the heavy pail of water.

A flying clod of dirt struck Paul on the shoulder suddenly, and Ora grinned down impishly at him.

"That was the lunch bell," she announced.

Bracha was ladling stew from a steaming cauldron onto tin plates. A few settlers were teasing her about the conquest she had made of a *Haganah* youth. Her strong buckteeth flashed in a good-natured smile.

"That Bracha!" Shlomo said, as Paul sat down beside him. "She could even make a stone taste good!"

"Don't tempt her to prove it," Paul said, watching Emmi eat her food with relish. She had the beaming look of a youngster at a picnic. Ora, he saw, was frowning. He followed her glance and saw three Arabs gesticulating angrily at Noah. The *Haganah* boys, with a deceptive casualness, moved closer.

Then Avram came over and squeezed in between Emmi and Dov. "They claim the markers are their *ma'asha* land," he said, in answer to Ora's questioning look.

"But our markers are a good ten *dunum* away from theirs!" Ora said.

"They look so angry," Emmi said. "Does it really matter — five *dunum* more or less — to us?"

"Let's make them a present of the five *dunum*," Avram said, with a hint of sarcasm in his voice. "Then they'll move their markers five *dunum* closer to ours and claim we're on *ma'asha* land. We'll give them the five *dunum*, and then five more, until we won't even have the ground under our feet left."

"You don't give in when you're in the right," Ora said dryly. "They'll think we're afraid of them, and the next time they won't come with demands — but with rifles."

Bracha had now ladled out the last of the stew and she came over with her plate. She sat down next to Emmi, dwarfing her with her big shoulders. She held her plate over Emmi's and slid some meat onto it, against Emmi's protests.

"I kept tasting while I cooked, so I'm not hungry," she said to Emmi, quietly. Her cheeks were flushed an apple red and she wiped the sweat from her face with a handkerchief. There was such a contented, good-natured look on her face that she imparted her sense of well-being to the others. They all loved her.

"The clearing for the cement house looks small," Dov observed. "I thought we were building one big dwelling for all."

"Who wants to live one on top of the other?" Bracha said. "There's no peace in it. With all the crowding, I feel like I'm married to the whole *kibbutz*."

"Then why haven't I been getting the benefits?" Dov demanded, grinning. Bracha hooked her arm tightly around his neck and shook him and he made such comical grimaces that Emmi burst into laughter.

"Don't strangle our conductor," she said, pulling at Bracha's arm.

"Not until after our first concert, anyway," Ora said. She got up as she saw Jehiel, at the outer fringe of the group, pick up his spade and return to work.

"But you do care what happens to me, Emmi — you do love me, don't you?" Dov asked teasingly, when Bracha released him.

"Oh, yes! I do love you and you will make a very, very good conductor!" Emmi said in great earnest, as she smoothed back his ruffled hair.

"Ah-ha" Dov exclaimed. "When a concert artist tells her conductor that she loves him, she only means that she wants a bigger slice of the program!"

How different the field looked, with most of the stones and brush cleared away in the sector where she worked, Emmi thought. Almost like the fields near Erlangen, just before the peasants began the plowing. Shlomo, swinging his scythe at the tall rushes, accentuated this feeling for her. She followed after him, piling the weeds into a heap to be burned.

As Emmi worked, her movements took on the flowing rhythm of a piece of music. All at once, the full orchestral glory of the "Ode to Joy" swelled up inside her. She remembered each note of the chorale, each word in praise of brotherhood, and wondered why they had not thought of including it in their program. She must ask Dov, and hurried off to the well site.

Suddenly, she stopped, frozen in her steps. Strange yells filled the air as Arabs came pouring down the hill, waving sticks. Someone — it was Noah, she could see the plume of white hair — went scrambling up the hill. The Arabs closed in on him, and Jehiel flailed out savagely with his fists. From every part of the fields, settlers were running up the slope with picks and spades.

Where to hide! Emmi thought. Where, in all this bare wilderness, could she hide? She stood transfixed with panic. The trucks! If she could crawl to the trucks — she would be safe.

Suddenly, a stone crashed at her feet. The Arabs must have seen her! More stones dropped around her then, and the Arabs' shrieks sounded louder, nearer — and fiercer. Any instant now, and they would seize her, she was certain. She lay flat on the ground, trembling and terrified.

It had been madness to volunteer! If she survived, she would take Erni and run off! This very night! Anywhere — perhaps the Germans at the Templar colony near Haifa would take pity on them. They had, after all, a common Fatherland in Germany.

She began crawling. The trucks were now near enough for her to make a hurried dash over to them. Suddenly, her hand touched a body, and she recoiled with a strangled cry. "Paul!"

His face, deathly white, was splattered with blood from a wound at his temple. Emmi leaned over and shook him. He moaned, and her heart leaped. He was alive! If she could get to the first-aid truck, she could save him.

The distance to the truck was less than a hundred yards, but to Emmi, it seemed to lengthen treacherously as she crawled. The crowd on the slope was a blurred mass in motion, now — surely, from that distance, they could not see her. Rising, she dashed over to the truck and snatched some bandages and a bottle of peroxide. Then, crouching low, she hurried back to Paul.

He was sitting up, holding his head with both hands. "Somebody clubbed me," he said, smiling weakly.

"Lie down!" Emmi said, excitedly. "I must clean the wound and dress it, but you must lie down or we will be seen."

"It's only a surface bruise," Paul said, as Emmi bandaged it carefully.

"What happened to you, Emmi?" he said. "I yelled for you to run to the trucks — I ran over to get you — but you'd vanished!"

Flushing guiltily, she finished binding his head, without answering.

Then unexpectedly, they heard laughter and sat up. The settlers had beaten off the Arabs! Dov came running over, his shirt dangling in shreds from his shoulders. His face was bruised but his eyes were feverish with excitement. "So you got your baptism!" he exclaimed, roughing Emmi's hair with his hand. "It could have been worse!"

Then Ora came striding across the field. She had lost her cap in the fighting, and the wind tossed her black hair against her face. She looked anxiously at Paul.

"How's Noah?" Paul asked.

"He's had a few knocks, but he's all right," Ora said, combing her hair with her fingers. "He's with the *mukhtar,* who claims it wasn't his villagers — but the Bedouins — who attacked."

"We should have fired a few shots," Dov said.

"We didn't come here to fight," Ora snapped back.

"If you don't want to fight, don't buy any more land!" Dov retorted, yelping as Emmi swabbed his bruised jaw.

The settlers were in high spirits as they climbed into the trucks for the ride back to Tel Hashava. They joked and sang, and Dov began a fast-paced patter song that amused everyone. Everyone — except Emmi. Had the attack really happened? she wondered. Could she have imagined the brutal fighting, the weird Arab shrieks, the shower of stones? But, no — there was Paul, with the bandage she herself had wound about his head. And Jehiel, with the white patch on his forehead. And Avram, with the angry welt near his eye! — And Bracha's head scarf was smeared with blood.

It *had* happened, Emmi knew, and it would be worse when the British left. Life on the hill would be dangerous if not fatal.

The group were singing now, their voices a dissonant roar in the cavern of the truck. Dov led them, calling out, "Who will build the Galilee..." And back, like a battle cry, "*We* will build the Galilee..."

It wasn't a song — it was a shouted challenge — and it jarred Emmi's nerves unbearably. The truck seemed like a cave closing in on her with this chant roaring inside her head. She got up and edged her way to the open end of the truck, gulping in air.

Leaping to his feet, Dov seized her just as she swayed outward. She shook him off with a little jab of her elbow and he shrugged, as though permitting her a tantrum after the tension of the attack. He half-turned to go back to his seat when something he saw startled him.

Emmi saw him frown and thought that she had offended him. He only meant to prevent her from falling out, she knew. Apologetically, she reached for his arm. Just as she did so, some shots rang out. Dov shuddered, then seized Emmi and quickly threw her to the floor, falling on top of her, to protect her. The truck lurched, and then rocked to a standstill.

Emmi heard shouts and at the same moment felt Dov's body jerk upward. She tried to wriggle from under him.

"Lie still!" he hissed in her ear.

She felt a warm, sticky wetness at her neck, and cried out softly, "Dov — you are hurt!"

"Don't be frightened, Emmi!" he said in German, as he struggled to his feet. Then he collapsed. Ora climbed into the truck, carrying the first-aid kit. The front of Dov's shirt was crimson.

"Don't move, Dov, or the bleeding will get worse," Ora said.

Avram came hurrying over. He looked anxiously at Dov and then questioned Ora with his eyes. She shook her head.

Dov's mouth worked to form a question, and Avram said, "No — it's not an attack. A few Bedouins went wild — our boys took care of them."

"Our boys are *gibborim*," Dov said. A lock of his hair hung across his forehead and, gently, Emmi smoothed it back. At her touch, the look of agony on his face disappeared, and a serene smile replaced it. Emmi leaned over and kissed him.

"You will be well! Oh, you will!" she cried.

"Those born to be hanged don't die of a bullet," Dov said with a crooked smile.

Emmi took his hand, kissed it, and pressed it to her cheek. His eyes lingered on her gratefully for a moment, then turned glassy. With a frightened cry, Emmi began to shake him.

"Don't, Emmi," Ora said tonelessly. "He is dead."

Emmi could feel the sticky wetness at her shoulder, that was Dov's blood, seep through her skin to her bones.

She did not know when they reached Tel Hashava, nor could she feel Avram lift her in his arms as he carried her to her tent.

Chapter Fourteen

It wasn't true — Dov was still alive! Emmi wouldn't have it otherwise. He was playing some kind of trick, teasing them, Emmi was sure. He was somewhere in the crowd at the grave, and any moment now, he would spring from among them with his devil-may-care grin and say something that would make them laugh.

The pine box being lowered was only a hoax — a trick — his usual way of scoffing at ceremony. Emmi craned her neck to catch the familiar sound of Dov's laughter. Jehiel was intoning a prayer. She turned away to leave, and Avram's hand on her arm tightened.

"Don't go," he whispered. "Jehiel is saying the prayer for the dead."

Impassively, Emmi looked about her. Everyone was so solemn and tearful. Shimon's face looked paler and bonier than ever. Dvora was swaying to and fro, making low, whimpering sounds. And it was strange to see Ora crying, with crystals of tears glistening on her bronzed cheeks. Paul's face was rigid, as if he were clenching his jaws. Noah's eyes were closed behind red, puffy lids. And Bracha, both hands holding her face, stood rigid about the others like a Niobe weeping for her slain.

"*El Mahleh Rahamin . . .*"

God is full of mercy . . .

The first few words of the remembrance of souls always moved Paul deeply, but now Jehiel's intoning of it evoked a raw and immediate pain. It was more than a prayer for Dov; it was a reminder of the ageless and unending oppressions that haunted all their lives. And it was the lament of Jews mourning, through their immediate dead, the slain of all Israel.

When the prayer ended, a silence fell on the settlers and they looked expectantly at Noah. He stood leaning over the grave, and began speaking, softly, feelingly, as if unburdening his heart to a beloved comrade. Then he turned to the other mourners and stood silently before them a moment while his eyes, dulled with pain, blinked back tears.

"We will not pay tribute to Dov by seeking vengeance — but rather by our works in rebuilding our homeland. For every comrade who falls, let us bring in hundreds from exile; let us build new *kibbutzim* for them. What happened yesterday happened all our yesterdays. We live in fear here, and elsewhere, but let us conquer this fear by strengthening our beliefs — our efforts . . ."

In the storehouse, Emmi stared vacantly at the torn linen in her hand. Distractedly, she threw it into the carton under the window. She wished that Shimon and Erni would leave her alone, but they kept shadowing her.

"Listen to me, Emmi," Shimon said as he followed her from the carton back to the table. "You will feel better if you cry. Do not lock your sorrow inside you. We are all crying — there is no shame in it."

But it wasn't shame that dammed up Emmi's tears. It was blood — Dov's blood on her had frozen them. If she hadn't gone to the open end of the truck, he would be alive today.

·164

"Don't tell her to cry!" Ernie shouted. "I don't want her to cry!" He glowered at Shimon.

"You must not speak boldly to someone older!" Emmi scolded. Erni nuzzled his head against her shoulder.

"Why are you not in school?" Shimon asked.

"There is no school because of Dov," Erni said.

The large carton was heaped with linen to be mended and here Emmi sat with idle hands! With a deep, shuddering sigh, she picked up her needle and began sewing. As she sewed, the confusions that had tangled her thoughts all through the night began to sort themselves into one clear wish.

"I want to return," she said gravely to Shimon.

Erni let out a yelp of joy.

"Return where" Shimon asked.

"Home. To Erlangen."

A faint smile flickered across Shimon's face. "You are no longer a child, to wish for the moon. Those who return find only hatred there now — as if we were responsible for the defeat, the ruins. I know this — it is only two months since I left Germany."

Erni's eyes widened. Shimon was a newcomer to Palestine! Why had Emmi lied to Alan about him?

"Then, I will go to England — or to America. Paul will help me get a visa." She said this softly, but her eyes met Shimon's with the determined look of an irrevocable decision.

"Do you think you are wanted there?" Shimon asked.

"But we are not wanted here, either!" Her voice broke. "I am seventeen years old — I must make a life for myself — and for Erni. I can't do this — here. I don't feel as though I belong . . ."

"You won't find yourself belonging there, either. When conditions are good, the Gentiles don't mind us — they even tolerate us — but when conditions are bad . . ." Shimon shrugged off the rest with one of his bitter smiles.

Erni hated him now. Shimon had won out — he could tell by Emmi's crushed look. He wished the Arabs had killed Shimon instead of Dov. It was very dull in the room now, he thought, with Emmi silent and bent over the mending. Erni saw Yigal and ran out to play with him.

With a sob, Emmi pushed her sewing away. "But why did it have to happen to our wonderful Fatherland?"

It was all too familiar — this cry — and Shimon sighed at the futility of an answer. Nothing he said could ease the pain of her *heimweh*.

"How long must we remember what happened?" Emmi asked brokenly. "Is it not time to forgive?"

Shimon's throat worked convulsively, as if it had suddenly filled with bile. "Emmi, go to Auschwitz, gather the ashes of your father and say, 'Father, you have been dead a long time. Is it not time to forgive those who murdered you?' "

Emmi shrank from Shimon's words as if he had struck her.

"Every age has its own evils," he went on, relentlessly. Emmi had to be bolstered with understanding, Shimon felt, so that her love for the Land might be strengthened. "What happened in Germany was the sum of all evil because Hitler tried to set up a devil's kingdom on earth. And the Germans let him! So they hate us more now, because we remind them of this evil. They will not forgive the Jews for the crimes *they* committed against *us*."

"But they hate us here, too. They will destroy us!" Emmi said.

"We will not be destroyed," Shimon replied. "We have survived Hitler, and we will not be destroyed here. Throughout history, the nation that has tried to doom the Jew has written its own doom, instead. Was it not said by Isaiah,

"Behold, they may gather together, but not by Me;

Whosoever shall gather together against thee shall fall because of thee!"

"But how can you have faith, after all that has happened?" Emmi asked. "What is it — this faith?"

"Without faith, man would still be living in a cave," Shimon said. "Man must have faith that good will prevail — otherwise, we lose the basis of our sanity — reason and hope."

Tilting back Emmi's face, Shimon looked deeply into her eyes as if to pierce the veil that was shrouding them. "Emmi," he said, "we are building a homeland where no one can make us afraid, or ashamed of being a Jew. That is why Dov came here. Don't desert him by your thoughts."

Shimon's words broke the ice at Emmi's heart. She dropped her face into her hands and began weeping.

Later, the dark thoughts that had been burdening Emmi closed in on her again. With Dov gone, the concerts — which only yesterday had been such a source of ecstasy — seemed like a dream, a bursting bubble that would leave no trace of itself. Now, there would be nothing but the drudgery of work, and loneliness. — And the terrible fears.

Erni and Yigal were sitting on the ground, their chins cupped in their hands. They were gazing at the low mound of earth before which the settlers had stood weeping only an hour before. Rina, their teacher, had told them about Dov and then had dismissed them. Dov, she said, would no longer amuse them with musical antics on his concertina — or teach them games — or tell them stories.

How lonely it was, here at the grave. And frightening,

too. Everyone was with someone, and Erni was glad that Yigal was with him. Yigal was his friend now. They became friends when Dov was teaching them games. In class, Yigal was very bright, but he was stupid when it came to learning games, Erni thought, and Erni had to help him catch on.

They had become close friends the previous week, when Rina had taken them to Haifa to the dentist. Yigal had refused to open his mouth so that a tooth could be pulled. Returning to the settlement, he had let Erni touch the loose tooth. It wiggled when Erni put his finger on it, and Erni knew that it would come out very easily just as his own tooth had, back home in Erlangen, when his friend Johan had jerked it out. Yigal sensed this, as Erni wiggled it, he squeezed both his eyes shut. When he opened them, there was the tooth — on the palm of Erni's hand! Yigal and Erni had laughed uproariously and had gone around showing off the tooth to everyone. Since then, they were friends.

But Yigal was sorry that Erni had come here with him. He wanted to be alone to think — and to watch. His stare was fixed hard on the grave, and he wondered if he was too late to see Dov's soul rising on the wings of the *Schechina* — the Divine Presence. He did not know if the soul left the body at the same time that the breath did — or when the body was laid in its temporary home, until the Messiah came. He had meant to ask his father about this, but he had stayed the night through beside Dov, praying.

It was getting tiresome, sitting here and doing nothing, Erni thought to himself. He nudged Yigal and held out a string, Yigal seized it eagerly, but then, thinking that Dov's soul might take flight while he was playing, he shook his head. Erni wondered why his friend looked so troubled, but he did not know the Hebrew words to ask him.

Below them, the police pickup was parked at the concrete building. How had he missed its arrival? Erni leaped to his feet and began running, waving his hand.

Karl was tinkering with the engine as Erni came over, and Erni felt shy about greeting him. Karl's moods were unpredictable. Either he scowled and looked as if he would cuff Erni, or else he called out a friendly hello. And sometimes, he would look right through Erni as if he weren't there at all! Erni edged closer, kicked at some pebbles, as he waited to be noticed.

Wiping his hands on a rag, Karl looked up and smiled at Erni. He nodded in the direction of the settlers, who were standing about in small groups, and asked, "Is it a Jewish holiday, or what?"

"Dov is dead," Erni said. "He was lots of fun — I liked him."

"And this other — the new one who came — do you like him too?"

"Shimon?" Erni scowled. "I hate him. He is always with Emmi."

"Shimon?" Karl said. "Is that the new one's name?"

Erni nodded, wondering why Karl darted away so abruptly.

The settlers seemed a downhearted lot, Alan thought, as he went over to the storehouse. They stood about with a doomsday look on their faces. Terrible thing — getting shot at — but as the captain said the night before, after the phone call from Noah, violence begets violence. The settlers ought not to have rushed to the hill.

And the captain had given Sgt. Cassidy the dickens for not checking up on illegal immigrants, as he had been detailed to do. Karl must have told on the sergeant.

The shooting yesterday had given him a scare, and he would have come to see Emmi last night but orders had come through to stop patrolling the roads. The captain had remained at the post and there was nothing Alan could do but stay there, worrying.

He would like to see Emmi well out of this place. He had no news for her about a job, but he would tell her to keep off that hill. The risks were too great...

Through the open door of the storehouse, Alan could see Emmi bent over her sewing. There were tears on her face and she looked so sad that he was overcome, for the moment, with pity for her. Glancing up, Emmi saw him, and the expression of joy that filled her face brought him to her in one swift movement. She loved him — he was sure!

"I am so happy you came! Oh, so happy!" she cried.

"There now — it's all over...."

"But it isn't," Emmi said. "It will get worse when we move there! Oh, it was dreadful... not even a place to hide. I can't go there... I just can't...."

"You don't have to, Emmi..." Alan said.

"You have found a place for me?" Her voice lifted excitedly.

"Well, not yet..." Then, impulsively, he blurted, "Emmi, why don't you marry me — and we can go off to England?"

The unexpectedness of his words, the uncertainty that she had heard right, made Emmi draw back. But Alan felt unable to control his emotions — his impulsiveness.

"I'll ship you off to my mother's until I'm through here — about six or seven months from now. She's a fine person — you'll like her. She's head nurse in the hospital there. And we have a home, not like the one you had, but it's comfortable. And I'll get work — I was a mechanic before I came here ..."

It was odd, Emmi felt, this mixture of joy and doubt — when she should have felt undivided joy. There was a feeling of unreality about what Alan was saying, as though all this was happening somewhere else — to someone else.

"Does — does your mother know about me?" she asked.

"I write to her. I didn't write about our getting married, though, because — well — I've only just asked. But she'll be pleased ..."

"Does — does she know that I am ... I mean, *what* I am ... ?"

"A Jew?" he asked. "She won't mind — she's tolerant that way."

Alan's words stabbed a fresh pain into an old wound. Emmi stiffened and drew away. "I do not like — being *tolerated!*" she said icily.

His face screwed up questioningly. "What do you mean?"

"I am what I am," Emmi said. "And I won't apologize for it. That is how I was made to feel when — when *they* tolerated me!"

"Don't, Emmi," he said. "Let's not have an argument before we're even married. I didn't mean what you think — it's all right, you being a Jew. It's how you behave that counts with me."

A fugitive smile touched Emmi's mouth and her face lost some of its hurt.

"There now, that's better. Look here, Emmi, this Arab business isn't over yet and won't be for some time. I want you well away from it. I can't marry you here — I'd be fired if I married a native .."

"But I am not one!" she protested.

"Once you are here legally, you are. I will send you and Erni to my mother. Then, when my service is up, we will get married. What do you say?"

"Oh, yes! Yes! I want to go to England!" she cried.

When Sgt. Cassidy came into the office, Paul looked up from his note-taking and questioned Noah with his eyes. Noah gestured for him to remain.

"Terrible thing, losing a lad like Dov," Cassidy said.

Noah seemed to have aged overnight; his cheeks were sunken, his eyes dull, and his body had lost its bounce.

With a heavy sigh, Cassidy lowered himself to a chair thinking it was a foolish thing, coming indoors, when what had to be done — rounding up the settlers for their identification cards — must be done outside. "Noah, I've just come from Um Tubas. The *mukhtar* swore that none of his people were mixed up in the shooting."

"He swears too easily," Noah said. "He told me the same thing, but Avram recognized several of his villagers in the attack on the bus. The shooting began on our way back . . . I want an investigation."

"Noah, the case is closed," Cassidy said.

"Closed! It hasn't even been opened yet!" Noah struck the desk with his fist. Paul looked up from his work, startled. It was the first time he had ever heard Noah explode in anger.

"We're not asking for protection — only justice," Noah insisted.

"Be sensible, Noah," Cassidy replied. "You will settle on the hill and all the British police won't be able to help, once you get a blood feud started . . ."

"And if we drop the matter . . .?" Noah broke in angrily. "The Arabs know the British won't make any ar-

·172

rests because the Mandatory doesn't care how many Jews are murdered — the hundreds of unsolved murders prove this. Do you think that will make it any safer for us?"

Cassidy went on doggedly, "And if partition is voted at the United Nations, this country will drown in blood."

"Partition shouldn't bother you," Noah said. "You'll get a job policing elsewhere — and then a pension . . ."

Cassidy snorted. "Pension, my eye. Less than a quid a week. They promised us a lifetime job with a decent pension at the end of it . . ." He swore under his breath. He'd served His Majesty's constabulary these past twenty years, and now he would be turned loose with a pension that wouldn't feed a dog.

If he weren't on in years, he had half a mind to ask Noah to take him on as a settler. That girl, Bracha, had been nagging him for years to do this and he'd always laughed her off. Nor would he be the first of the constables to do this, either. He'd heard of a dozen already and even more soldiers had joined. He'd like to see Bracha's face the day he turned up in *mufti*. He restrained the smile that had started across his face.

Now, Cassidy had to face up to the grimmest part of his duty. He put on his official scowl. "Noah, line up the settlers — every one of them. I want to see their cards."

Unnoticed, Paul slipped out of the room, thankful that Cassidy's broad back was to the door. Outside, he collided with Karl.

Erni, waiting at the pickup, could see the door of the office open as Paul came out. He watched as Paul bumped into Karl, almost knocking him down. Paul headed for the vegetable garden behind the building just as Shimon went limping over toward the sheds near the barn. Then Cassidy came out of the office with Karl and Noah.

The three looked angry. It would be pointless to wait for Karl, Erni decided.

Yigal was still sitting near Dov's grave when Erni returned. "Let's play," Erni said, in the few Hebrew words Dov had taught him. He held out a string. With a resigned sigh, Yigal looped it around his hands. It was useless to watch for Dov's soul to make its ascent. It must have left his body when he died, Yigal decided.

Somehow, his fingers were being stupid today, Erni felt. He gnashed his teeth when neither the boat nor the cradle would take shape from the string. But his mind wasn't really on the game. He felt nervous and wished that he hadn't mentioned Shimon's name to Karl. If Emmi lied to Alan, she had her reasons, Erni knew, because Emmi *never ever lied!*

Erni tangled the string and, with a savage pull, broke it. His heart felt heavy, just as it used to feel back home when he did something naughty. He hadn't meant to tell on Shimon — his words just came out, without his even thinking about it. He dropped his head on his arms and, suddenly, began to sob. Watching him, and weighed down by all the sadness, Yigal put his arm around Erni and began to cry softly.

Emmi felt a cozy intimacy as Alan folded the mended sheets for her while they talked. It was almost as if they were married already! She got up to get more linen from the carton when she spotted Shimon crouching behind the rear wall of the machine shed. His face was ashen and his eyes glazed with terror.

He had been found out!

Instinctively, Emmi stood with her back to the window so that Alan would not see him. If she could somehow signal Shimon to get to Boulder Hill!

The sound of feet running on gravel — the shouting — sent panic through her. Shimon had been seen! The other constable was after him now! Alan got up and started out. Emmi clutched his arm but he wrenched it free. Outside, the settlers were shaking their fists at someone in the machine shed — cursing and jeering. Karl ran out and made a dash for the barn. Dvora, standing at the door, jabbed a pitchfork menacingly at him.

"He's armed! He's in there!" Karl shouted, as Alan came running over. Emmi stood outside the storehouse, helplessly wringing her hands. Shimon was trapped!

The crowd surged forward. Avram elbowed his way through to Alan. "He isn't armed. Let me go in ... I'll talk to him," he said, following Alan to the barn.

"You keep away!" Dvora shrieked, threatening Alan with the pitchfork.

Cassidy came striding down the street with Bracha running alongside him, pleading, "We've lost one man — let Shimon stay in his place ... Cassidy ... listen to me! Let him stay!"

"Let him stay!" The settlers took up Bracha's cry as they swarmed around Cassidy. Then Cassidy was blocked in as if by a living wall. Karl and Alan struggled to reach him but they, too, were hemmed in by the wall of settlers.

Suddenly, Shimon darted out the barn. He looked frantically about him, then saw Emmi motioning him to the rear of the storehouse.

The carton! She would hide him in it! She hurried inside and began emptying it. She would heap the linen over him — they would search the settlement and not think of looking for him here!

Emmi shuddered each time the pebbles of gravel crunched under Shimon's feet. She leaned out of the window and reached for him — he was within touching distance now.

All at once, a great shout — a screamed warning — broke out as Alan came running over to the storehouse. Shimon stood paralyzed. His eyes had the terror-crazed look of a trapped animal. Then he wheeled around and ran, his arms flailing the air wildly.

Alan lunged at him. Shimon struggled to pull free, but Alan felled him with a blow. Then he dragged the limp figure to the pickup.

Emmi watched as if in a trance. Then, with a cry, she ran over to Alan and screamed, "You Nazi! You vile Nazi!"

Alan flung his prisoner onto the pickup and climbed in. He sat stiffly erect with his rifle across his knees. The settlers crowded around the vehicle, shouting their curses. Bracha stood staring at Cassidy, without speaking. Only her eyes spoke, and Cassidy felt himself damned.

Chapter Fifteen

The cloud of dust that enveloped the police pickup as it left the *kibbutz* had hardly settled when the shouts of defiance began to subside. The sudden change in Cassidy, the brutality with which Shimon had been seized, filled everyone with foreboding. They had considered Cassidy their friend and protector and he had unmasked himself as the enemy.

It was as if everyone felt Shimon's fate to be theirs, they would all be slaughtered. "It's all the same to me, whether I live or die," Dvora sobbed. Her face was twisted with grief. "If they kill a saint like Shimon ..."

"They won't kill him," Emmi said, putting her arms around Dvora. "They only arrested him."

Dvora wiped away her tears with the back of her hand. "His wisdom shone like a light on his face. No one was so stupid that he could not learn from Shimon. Me, the dumb cow, even to me he talked of poetry, philosophy ..."

Emmi could understand but little of Dvora's outpouring, but she understood her grief. Through the window of the barn, she saw Ora and Avram moving briskly toward Boulder Hill. Jehiel, then Paul, then Shlomo followed. And then Bracha.

"Where are they going?" Emmi asked.

"To practice self-defense," Dvora answered, shaking off some wisps of hay that clung to her dress. "Emmi, you are different than I thought," she said pensively. "No wonder Shimon loved you like a daughter." She embraced Emmi and then went out.

As she moved past the window, Emmi hurried after her. "I want to go, too," she said. "I want to be helpful."

"Where are you going?" Ora demanded, seeing Emmi.

Emmi braced her shoulders and met Ora's look with a hint of defiance. "To learn self-defense!"

Her answer was not as much a reply as it was a challenge and Ora felt pleased by it. With a nod, she turned and strode ahead. Dvora linked her arms in Emmi's and they fell in line behind the others. Then Bracha turned and gave Emmi's arm a squeeze. "Good!" she said. "It is good to know how to defend yourself. Then you have no fear."

Taking long steps to keep pace with Bracha, Emmi thought about what she had just said. She was not sure that knowing how to protect herself would banish her fears. She only knew that the settlers were one big family and that she could not bear to be an outsider.

Ora could see Hassan's red roadster as she came down Boulder Hill late that afternoon and she ran the rest of the way to the settlement. He must have heard about Dov and the hill fighting over the radio and was worried about her. The thought that he would come now, after their bitter quarrel, cheered her and she hurried even faster.

His arms folded, Hassan was standing at the office window as Ora entered, a morose look on his face. Her heart jolted as his look fell on her unseeingly and then shifted. He doesn't even sense that I am here! she thought.

Tonelessly, Noah was describing the events on the hill to Nourse. The journalist rose when Ora came in, and they shook hands. Hassan remained at the window but Ora caught the quick caress of his eyes as he glanced briefly at her — the guarded smile.

He is a man divided, she thought. He is afraid of being branded a traitor to the Arab cause and he is anguished for me. Oh, how reluctantly he loves me. Almost as though he hates me for being what I am.

Avram and Paul followed Ora into the office. Neither Hassan nor Avram made a move to greet each other, but nodded coldly.

"Had enough?" Nourse asked, when Paul greeted him.

"I'm not ready to call it quits, if that's what you mean," Paul said, surprised at how relieved he felt to see the American.

" Exactly what I mean," Nourse grinned. "The ships are jammed with Americans rushing home."

"But why are they leaving?" Noah asked.

"Because there's unholy terror in the holy land that — come partition — can lead to war," Nourse offered.

"Come off it, Nourse," Avram said, waving his hand disparagingly. "You are confusing weather with climate. Tourists always leave around this time. They come for the High Holy Days and then leave when the rains set in."

"Mr. Nourse isn't confusing the weather with the climate," Hassan said quietly. "He has seen the anti-Zionist demonstrations and he knows the climate is violence. There will be war if the United Nations decides on partition."

"But why, Hassan?" Ora asked. "Why? We have been living peacefully with the Arabs in this vicinity — we've been helpful . . ."

"Too helpful, the Arabs say," Nourse broke in. "They tell me you've helped yourselves to their land . . ."

"You've been taken in by the Arab press," Avram said hotly.

"That's nonsense!" Nourse's eyes snapped angrily. "I've been strictly neutral!"

"Neutral!" Paul broke in. "I've read some of your pieces. *mufti* hand-outs — with a Tad Nourse by-line!" He stood leaning against the wall, his shoulders hunched — hands jammed in his pockets. His lean face was tight with anger.

Ora's eyes widened. Paul was actually taking sides *against* his own countryman! She had been standing near him with her elbows propped on a roll-top desk, but now she straightened and her shoulders touched his. Paul looked at her knowingly. Watching them, Hassan's face hardened.

With a reproving look at the three youths that warned them to control their tempers, Noah turned to Avram and said admonishingly, "Mr. Nourse is a reputable journalist. I do not think he would accept the word of a Hitler Arab. One's sympathy can be with the Arabs as ours is — but we can also see when they are misled . . ."

"And when are they misled?" Hassan said edgily. "When they see new immigrants taking their jobs away, or when they see new settlements rising on their ancient lands? If you Zionists had been satisfied with a limited, fixed immigration, there would have been no trouble."

Outraged and shocked at Hassan's words, Ora gasped. She wondered if anything could be more crushing than hearing one's beloved speak like the enemy.

"But they kept lowering the quota . . ." Avram said indignantly.

"Patriotic Palestineans would do almost anything rather

than yield to Zionist demands for a higher immigration quota," Hassan answered sharply.

"Patriotic Palestineans!" Ora retorted. Her voice was sarcastic. "Hassan, you don't know how comical you sound! The Arab has no national patriotism — only *tribal* loyalty! The only real patriotism this country knows is the patriotism *we've* had for two thousand years!"

Shaking his head in a hopeless gesture, Hassan crossed the room. He paused before Nourse and said bitterly, "Now you know why peace is not possible. If *friends* can't come to terms, what do you expect of the others? I'll wait for you in the car." He walked over to the door and opened it. Pausing briefly, he turned to Noah. "Don't go up the hill land, Noah," he said. "There is sure to be trouble."

Ora could feel her heart beat, her pulse, her breath, all stop as Hassan passed her with a look that said she had ceased to exist for him.

The greyness of dusk was setting in when Ora left the others in the office. Her head ached unbearably. A pearly mass of clouds hung over Boulder Hill and the peacefulness beckoned her. Only there could she find the solitude she needed to ease the turbulence she felt.

Her mind was void of all thought as she started toward the hill. She felt only a heart-weary heaviness that grew more unbearable with every step. Dimly, she noticed that the dugout begun at the eucalyptus grove had been left unfinished. A spade lay on the mound of dirt. The settlers must have stopped digging when she sent word summoning everyone to the self-defense drill. She thought of resuming the work herself and was bending to pick up the spade when, suddenly, someone seized her and swung her around. It was Hassan! His eyes had the wild look of a madman.

She wrenched herself free and gave him a violent push as he called her a vile name.

"I've seen the looks the American gave you," Hassan said gruffly. "He must be laughing at the Arab you discarded for him!"

"You idiot! You stupid idiot!" she cried, striking him.

Hassan touched his cheek, his eyes blazing with fury. Ora backed away but he lunged at her, holding her with his arms. She struggled to free herself. Then, pulling back, she looked at him with such pity that a sob escaped him and he dropped his head on her shoulder.

Passively, she let his arms enclose her. She felt shattered by the sound of his sobbing and wanted to murmur an endearment. But she was too emotionally spent to find the right word. Finally, she said, "You are tormenting yourself over something that never happened, Hassan."

The sudden honk of a car horn startled them. Ora touched Hassan's arm gently and said, "Some day, perhaps, we will come together in love, Hassan." Then she walked quickly away.

That night, Ora and Emmi tossed sleeplessly on their cots. For Emmi, the day had begun in a haze of unreality. She kept remembering Dov's burial and imagined him flitting about mocking his mourners. But reality had come sharply into focus with Shimon's panic-stricken face as Alan seized him and struck him down.

She remembered Alan saying to her, in Haifa, "You are the best thing that's happened to me here," and had only to recall his words to feel them as pervasive and uplifting as a kiss. But, later, she had felt no joy when he had offered to marry her. Instead, she had the odd feeling that his proposal was being made to someone else.

Why did the words "she won't mind" keep echoing inside her, Emmi wondered. They had stabbed at some old wound and now, in her anguish of remembering, its scab had opened again.

Her music master had withdrawn her name from the student concert that was to be held in Nürnberg. "There might be complications," he had explained in a pained apology. Then, to soften the blow, he had listed her for the important musical event of the year in Erlangen annual subscription concert for the Children's Hospital.

Emmi had worked hard on the program, she remembered, and on the morning that she had rehearsed it for her teacher, he had leaned back on his chair, his arms folded, head lowered, and nodded — a sign that he was pleased. When she came to the Chopin Second Etude in F Minor, she knew, by the sudden tilt of his head, that she had achieved exactly the effect he wanted.

In the adjoining room, the chairlady of the concert had sat waiting for Herr Prof. Mahler. When he finally appeared, she had gushed her praise of the pianist until she saw that it was Emmi. Then her exuberance subsided. "They won't mind, I think," she had said. But they did mind — and Emmi had not played.

What, actually, had been her bond with Alan, Emmi wondered. Until only a few hours ago, it had been a feeling that she belonged more to the people of his world than with the settlers of Tel Hashava. Now, she felt that she could never see him again without feeling shattered by the blow he had struck Shimon. As she wept silently, she could hear Ora's deep, smothered sob.

Hassan would return — he must! It wasn't to ease the hurt, Ora assured herself, that he would return — it would simply be incredible for him not to! Sustained anger was contrary to his nature. How often, in the past — when they had lived in the Jezreel Valley — had he flared up and stalked away after a quarrel that seemed final and irreconcilable, only to return later. And, fiercely proud as he was, he would not utter a word of apology as he resumed working in the fields with her.

But Ora knew that Hassan's failure to return tonight meant that this time the break was final. She clutched at her pillow, pressing her mouth against it to smother the sob that escaped her.

"Ora, are you not well?" Emmi asked, leaning over her.

There was no answer. Emmi started back to her cot when she heard the strangled sob again. She touched Ora's shoulder lightly. "Can I get you something? A glass of water, perhaps?"

In the beam from the searchlight that swept across the floor, Emmi could see Ora's face twisted with grief. She knelt beside her and pressed her cheek against Ora's. After awhile, Ora sat up and wiped her eyes.

"How could he have looked at me like that?" The words came out brokenly between fresh sobs.

Emmi did not know what to say. Gently, she stroked Ora's hair.

"He always returned — the very same day — whenever we quarrelled before. I can't bear it — that he didn't come back tonight."

"Perhaps he will come tomorrow," Emmi said consolingly.

"No," Ora said, shaking her head. "It is no longer simply a quarrel between Hassan and me. It is his people against mine."

"Mine" — and not "ours." Emmi winced. Had Ora deliberately excluded her because of Alan? Her hand dropped from Ora's shoulder.

"I — I didn't mean that, Emmi. You aren't really going off with Alan, are you? We love you — don't leave us."

"I could never go off with him. I would always see him striking Shimon. And Shimon was like a father to me."

Ora put her arms around Emmi, and the two girls clung together and wept. Finally, Ora said, "We must try to sleep. There is the new field planting tomorrow . . "

Kissing Ora, Emmi returned to her cot. She felt comforted, with a warm feeling spreading through her at the thought that Ora and she were close friends at last. She fell asleep and slept so heavily that a sound of gunfire failed to rouse her.

Chapter Sixteen

The noise of gunshots awakened Paul from a fitful sleep. Dazed, he sat up and listened. They were being attacked! Hurriedly, he put on his clothes and then snatched the rifle which, since the noon drill, had lain under his cot. Crouching low, he ran to the dugout to which he had been assigned.

When he reached it, Avram was already firing at spurts of light on the opposite hill. Paul took aim and fired.

"Get down!" Avram hissed. Paul dropped to his knees and crawled to the dugout. More than the shooting, the weird yells that sounded in the distance unnerved him. Beads of sweat began trickling down his forehead. He fired a round of bullets before he was aware of hurried blows on his shoulder.

"Stop!" Avram was shrilling into his ear. "They've stopped shooting. Don't waste the ammunition." A sudden feeling of relief mixed with chagrin came over Paul. All lights had been extinguished and an inky darkness blotted out the village. A wave of dark clouds scuttled across the sky and a long golden spear probed the hills across the road like a spectral finger as Noah worked the searchlight. Crickets began their shrill, staccato whistling.

"I thought the Arabs in the adjacent villages were friend-ly," Paul said.

"They are," Avram replied. "The raiders are from across the border — the ones Cassidy warned us about, last week."

A fresh hail of shots silenced them again. Then an unearthly scream broke out and, above it, a high-pitched whinnying could be heard.

"They hit the stable," Avram said. "Hold your fire until they shoot." He crawled out of the dugout.

The crunching of pebbles under Avram's feet sound-ed like a spatter of shots on a tin roof. Paul tensed. The noise might direct fire toward Avram. The youth must have thought so, too, for presently he moved over to the soft turf of the lawn.

The silence lengthened. In it, every sound — the croaking of frogs, the crickets chirping, the wind stirring the stubble of wheat, even the scurrying of field mice — seemed ominously magnified to Paul. His own breath-ing sounded loudest of all, like the wheezing of rusty bellows.

What was he doing in a dugout, with a rifle? He had come here to observe, not to participate; he was a stu-dent doing research for his doctoral dissertation. His of-fer to join in the drill, after Shimon's arrest, had been merely a token gesture. He had not thought beyond it to the reality of fighting.

Looking back on that gesture, Paul knew that he had acted on two impulses, a desire to do something — any-thing — to lift the morale of the settlers and his wish to win Ora's approval. Actually, when she had summoned them for the drill, he could do nothing else but join. He had relished his own bravado when the settlers praised him, and Ora had given him one of her rare, beguiling smiles. But now, sweating it out because of the gesture, he cursed himself for a fool.

The crunching of footsteps near the dugout gave Paul a start and he fingered the trigger of his rifle. In the dark, he could make out a lean, bearded figure. He held his breath.

"*Shalom! Hacol beseder!*"

Peace. Everything okay. It was Jehiel, with news that the attack was over. Paul let out his breath in relief.

When he awoke the next morning, he felt oddly exhilarated. The settlers, too, were in a good mood. He heard it in the lift of their voices as they joked about the attack, and in the gay jabbering of the girls in the dining hall. But Paul thought their spirits were recklessly optimistic.

No one had been wounded. The animals were safe, although nervous, but several walls had been riddled and a few windows in the school hut shattered. The only casualty was Miriam, the kindergarten teacher, who had been cut by flying slivers of glass. Even the children were in high spirits as they scrambled about looking for shells.

The raid had tapped submerged resources of courage in everyone — particularly Emmi. Breathless with excitement, she cried, "Paul! I am to take charge of the kindergarten! Noah asked me! And he wants me to give the children piano lessons. Only . . . only . . ." Her face clouded. "Only they will laugh at the way I speak *Ivrith.*"

"Don't worry! When you run out of Hebrew words, just throw some musical terms at them!" Paul said, grinning.

Emmi giggled. "Ora said the same thing! And this morning, she taught me "Frère Jacques" in *Ivrith!* It sounds..." She stopped speaking as Noah came by and gave her an affectionate pat on her shoulder.

Paul was shocked at how haggard Noah looked. His eyes were bloodshot, encircled by dark puffs of wrinkled flesh. Only he — of all the settlers — looked as if he had spent the night in troubled sleeplessness. Perhaps he had less reason than the others to be optimistic, Paul thought.

At the United Nations that week, the debate on partition began. The reaction was swift and ominous. Arabs began attacking in broad daylight, and the radio was kept going continuously, at Tel Hashava.

Despite the alarming news and suspense over the outcome of the debate, the settlers were in an optimistic mood as they started out that morning to work the vineyard on the north field. They walked in pairs and in small groups. Paul could see rifles slung across backs — Ora's, Avram's, Jehiel's, Shlomo's. They were taking no chances.

The new planting began at the rocky ledge of Boulder Hill and sloped gently to the eucalyptus grove, which was marked off from the *wadi* and the Arab fields by a wire fence, newly erected.

Their light-hearted mood left the settlers as soon as they began digging holes for the slips and the saucer-shaped rings to hold water. It had turned cold. The workers were wearing jackets over their denim trousers and the girls had bright scarves on their heads.

Watching them, as he carried the containers of seedlings from the wagon, it seemed to Paul as if they were performing a pastoral dance: the downward thrust and lift of their spades, the bending to insert the slips, the forward step to the next planting — all in one unbroken, rhythmic flow of motion, their faces intent on purposeful work. They were all serious workers, Paul reflected. The lazy type, or the parasite, would find no place for himself in a *kibbutz*.

Here, in a microcosm, one could almost see the history of the Jews since their long exile from Palestine. They were all of the same racial stock and yet they had more in common, physically and psychologically, with the people of the countries in which they were born, than with each other in Tel Hashava.

Emmi was pure German in appearance and outlook, with her yearning for the *gemütlich*; and Dov's temperament had the gay abandon and the moody, cynical despair of his Hungarian compatriots. And like them, he was capable of noble gestures of futility. What had he in common with Jehiel, on whom the Yemenite Arabs had put the stamp of their backwardness?

Most of the settlers had in common the experience of rejection and persecution — and they had a bond of racial, historic memories. They were a nation of refugees!

The work, the close living together, the griping, the three-fold struggle of man — against himself, against nature and against the danger of attack — was fusing the settlers into a cohesive group that was beginning to acquire the solidity of nationhood.

Paul felt intrigued by the challenge of all this human material around him, and he hoped that reason — or a plague! — would overtake the Arab raiders so that he could get on with his research.

A visitor came that afternoon, announced by the clatter of horse hoofs. The settlers working in the field that paralleled the road could see the cloaked Arab, and they glanced nervously at each other, tightening their grips on the handles of their spades. In the glare of the sun, Bracha hooded her eyes and cried, "It is Abu Sa'id!" She ran to open the gate for him.

Noah rushed out of the office to greet his Arab friend as he swung himself down from his horse with the agility of a youth.

"*Shalom!*" Noah cried, embracing him.

"*Salaam Eleichum!*" Abu Sa'id responded. Then neither spoke as they went into the office. Closing the door, Noah could see Bracha running toward the dining hall. Ach — that jewel of a girl! In no time at all, she would bring coffee!

"Have you heard what happened?" Noah asked Abu Sa'id, after inquiring about his health and that of his family.

"The news brought me," the Arab said dourly.

He had heard and yet he came! Noah's eyes moistened with emotion. Then, because his friend looked pityingly at him, he cried out, "Who are they — these bandits who yell *'itbah lel Yahud!'* In the past, when we were attacked — your village as well as mine in the Jezreel — no one cried 'kill the Jew!' All they wanted was plunder, the normal Bedu grudge against the villager."

"*Fawzi el din Kawkji* will take up another man's cry, if there is gold enough," Abu Sa'id remarked dryly. "But the attackers last night are of another kind, altogether."

"Who are they?" Noah demanded. "We are on our own dearly bought land. It was purchased from Mahmoud el Shukhary. And no one lived here before — not even a hut was standing. There was swampland where it wasn't under stones. Surely, you remember?"

Abu Sa'id nodded. "It is not this land that makes the strife. It is the *partition,* that comes from outside. Our people want Palestine — all of it — not part of it."

Then, because Noah's face went blank with dismay, the old Arab looked away, troubled. A silence, heavy with unease, weighted the air. The next words, unwisely uttered, would tear a lifelong bond irrevocably past mending.

"It is said you are settling on *ma'asha* land," Abu Sa'id said, finally. "The *mukhtar* of Um Tubas swore this to me."

"He swears falsely," Noah replied. "We want nothing more than that our two villages be friendly, as ours were, in the valley."

"One cannot slaughter a cow and milk it at the same time," Abu Sa'id said. "You cannot have their land *and* their friendship."

Noah threw up his hands in exasperation. "But I told him we are leaving *ma'asha dunum* untouched, even though the court decided it was ours. But we must be left in peace to work the rest."

"Our people lived in peace in the old days because one did not swallow what did not belong to him. Now — wherever one looks — one finds a new settlement."

"But the *effendi* is well paid! Many times over! The land can hold us all! And more — many more! In ancient times, it fed five million! Now, there is scarcely a million. The Jews who return bring skills — everyone benefits..."

"But even the English — your friends — say..."

"*Our friends!*" Noah spat out the word. "Our friends take away our rifles — our friends refuse to stir, to come to our aid! If they are so concerned about our swallowing the land, why don't they sell us *crown* land — which lies in waste! *Our friends!*" With a thumbs down gesture of contempt, he added, "God save us from such friends. Our enemies, we can handle ourselves."

"But Noah, is it wise to press so hard? A slow pace reaches a surer goal."

"There is no time! Our people are rotting in camps still bloody with our dead. They are doomed unless they come here."

Abu Sa'id shook his head. "That is a cry I have heard before, Noah. It is the Zionist way to alarm, so that others will yield. But it alarms our people even more, and so there is strife. There will be war if partition is voted."

Had this been said by anyone else, Noah would have resigned himself to the futility of further discussion. But his old friend was not arguing from the enemy's camp — only from the enemy's position. Still, Noah felt no rancor. They had not always seen eye to eye from their earliest boyhood, but their disparate views had never weakened the firm bond of their friendship.

With a sigh, Noah asked, "Was there a Hitler?"

"*Walla! Walla!* He was *shaitan* on earth."

"The devil, exactly. Had he vowed to exterminate my people?"

"So he had spoken."

"And so he nearly did. How much longer can his survivors live on despair?"

"Allah alone knows each man's fate."

"But is not brotherhood one of Allah's precepts?"

The Arab nodded.

"Then how can we be deaf and blind to the distress of our brothers who pray to come to this land? How can you say we are pressing too fast? Hitler spoke in Berlin — and now our hills echo his threat — *itbah lel Yahud!* And the *mufti* is one with Hitler. My people plead with yours for peace — how, then, can you be deaf to our prayer? Is it not better to live in peace than to rot in death?"

"Some day, all people will come to know this — may Allah will it in our time."

Bracha came in with a tray of coffee. Her face had a strained look as she put the tray down on the desk and then quickly withdrew.

Noah knew that she had heard the argument and was frightened. These were sad days they had come upon — to live in fear of even an old friend. He sighed heavily as he poured the thick, black sweetened coffee into the tiny porcelain cups which Bracha kept for special visitors.

After the third ceremonial cup, the Arab rose. "I came only to bring you these for Dov's blood that is on my kinsmen's hands." Throwing back his *abayah* and loosening his girdle, he reached for something that was tied to his back. He pulled out two rifles and an ammunition belt.

Noah felt a gratitude too deep for utterance, and tears began filling his eyes. He put his hand on his friend's shoulder.

"You had best hide them," the Arab cautioned. "Or it will be prison if the English find more than you're legally entitled to."

"It is said that prison is no more than a station in our road to freedom," Noah answered, smiling wryly.

"It is a wise saying, but foolish for one to test it." Abu Sa'id arranged his robes and took leave of his friend. "We are old men, Noah, and Allah alone knows the time still due us. But these years will be as lifeless as dust if we do not counsel our young that only in the friendship that is peace, does man prosper."

"From your mouth to God's ear," Noah said fervently.

They embraced and then looked long and piercingly into each other's eyes as the same question haunted their thoughts. Would the other be alive to greet the morning?

That night, the alarm went off early. As Paul ran to his post, a bullet sank into the wet ground with a thud. He jumped into the dugout and found Jehiel already there.

"That was only a single shot," Paul said. "Either we are too early, or our visitors have been delayed."

"We are ready and waiting," Jehiel replied.

Of all the Hebrew-speaking settlers, Paul liked best to hear the Yemenite. The others' speech was guttural, while Jehiel's had a resonance that sounded like chanted poetry. Someday, Paul would ask Jehiel to chant the "Song of Songs."

"The children are in good spirits," Jehiel said. "They are happy with the music that Emmi teaches them. My Yigal worried over the strange little marks, but the boy, Erni, drew lines with letters for each line and the space between. I listened and I, too, know them!" He chuckled softly.

A rustle of movement silenced him. Jehiel crawled out of the dugout and Paul could hear a brief exchange of whispers.

"*Shelanu!*" Jehiel said, when he returned.

One of ours. A beautiful and comforting phrase. Paul wondered that Jehiel, a religious man, would fight on the Sabbath Eve, and the question was beginning to form on his lips when shots crackled. One of them whizzed past so close that Paul felt a knifelike rush of wind against his cheek and he shivered.

The chattering of Jehiel's rifle steadied him, and he took aim. In the moving beam of the searchlight, he could see a cloaked figure, his arms outspread, scrambling down the hill. Impaled in the light, the Arab was shocked to a standstill. Paul fired and the Arab hurtled down the hill to the field, where he lay motionless. Paul kept firing as fingers of steel pinched his cheek.

"Stop shooting!" Jehiel rasped. "We fire only to answer theirs. We can't waste ammunition."

It began raining, a leisurely patter that fell obliquely against the parapet and dripped into the dugout. Avram came over with orders to quit. "They don't fight in the rain. Besides, they were only probing our periphery defenses."

"*Yihye Tov. Shabbat shalom!*" Jehiel intoned.

Everything will be all right. Peace to the Sabbath.

Suddenly, Paul weakened with nervousness. He wished he could run the rest of the way to his tent, instead of keeping pace with Jehiel's sedate, even, walk.

That Sabbath morning, Jehiel's "congregation" was larger than usual. The small synagogue barely held all those who crowded into it. When the prayers were over, they went into the dining hall for the noonday meal. Bracha poked her head out of the kitchen, seeking out Jehiel with her eyes, and asked, "*Nu,* and did you pray us into a State?"

Jehiel smiled shyly as he nodded.

At the United Nations, the voting on partition had already begun. The settlers gathered around the radio in the dining hall and Bracha was kept busy, serving tea.

This did not relieve the suspense, but it eased the waiting.

Even Emmi, who until then had given scant thought to the happenings at Lake Success, was caught up in the suspense. She sat next to Avram on the bench, thinking, if we get a state of our own, surely the Arabs will respect us and will cease their attacks.

Suddenly, the radio went dead. Paul pounded it with his fist and over a crackling and sputtering, a voice announced, "Results at Lake Success: Thirty-three for partition, thirteen against, eleven abstentions, one absent. . ."

A stunned silence followed — everyone sat without moving, as though in a trance — then Ora broke the silence with a cry, "A state of our own!"

Bracha began weeping and Noah threw his arms around her and whirled her about. Avram pulled Emmi to her feet and, seizing Ora, the three danced around Noah and Bracha. The others flung themselves into a *hora,* stomping and singing and gathering in more settlers as they whirled about. They snatched at Jehiel, and tore Paul away from the radio.

It was more than a rejoicing; it was a wild eruption of the spirit, like nothing Paul had experienced before. And it had hysteria in it — for they were celebrating the rebirth of their nationhood. It was very late before the settlers ceased their dancing that night.

The rain came down hard all the next day. Erni watched it streaking from the roof in slanted lines that swelled the pool outside the building and stirred it into concentric circles. Beside him, Yigal stood counting the circles as they formed.

"To bed!" called out the housemother, switching off the light. Dutifully, and without bidding Yigal good-night, Erni went to bed. Emmi had not come by to say good night. The settlers were still celebrating the news about their new state, but that was not the reason she did not come. Something had happened between them that made Erni very unhappy. He felt that at any time now, something very dreadful was going to happen to him because he had told on Shimon.

That other night, when the shooting had broken out and the housemother had hurried into the room and ordered them all to lie down on the floor, he was certain the dreadful thing was about to happen. He had rolled under his cot and lain there trembling, with a fist in his mouth, but the next morning, everything was all right.

The children made a game of looking for the gun shells. Erni had been afraid to touch them but Yigal had put one in his hand and after that, he went looking for others. He thought it very odd that the shells were harmless in one's hand and yet could kill when they were fired from a gun.

The night before, he had slept through without once having to lie down on the floor. Perhaps the Arabs were afraid now, because the Jews were going to have a state! And perhaps what had happened to Dov and to Shimon had been only a dreadful dream and one day he would find Dov playing his concertina and dancing, as before. And perhaps Shimon would be in the storehouse with Emmi!

Everything would be exactly as it had been — only much much better because now he would be good about Shimon being with Emmi. He fell asleep with this consoling thought. He had not been asleep long when a crash rocked his cot, awakening him with a start.

"Erni, Get down!" Yigal screamed at him.

Frozen with fright he could not move. The dreadful thing he had been afraid of was beginning to happen! He would die — he knew it. He burrowed deeper under the blanket.

Yigal crawled over and pulled at his legs and Erni tumbled to the floor. He rolled under his cot and curled up tightly with his arms covering his head. He whimpered, but stopped when Yigal crept in beside him.

They clung together. Neither cried, but their teeth kept chattering.

Earlier that night, when the rain had ceased and Avram was assigning their posts, Paul demanded that the police or the Teggart Fortress be called on for help. "You are entitled to protection! What are you paying taxes for!"

"But we did telephone! They didn't come!" Avram replied.

"And if they do come, they'll only search us," Ora said crossly. "They'll make a shambles of the *kibbutz* if they find more rifles than we're legally entited to. It will mean prison for us . . ."

"It's pretty phony heroics, if you ask me — sweating it out every night — when we could demand . . ." Paul snapped in exasperation.

"You are free to leave for safety, if you wish," Ora replied. "After all, you are here only to observe."

Outside, Paul stumbled against Bracha. Jehiel was with her and they were humming Noah's song. They were on their way to the farthest outpost which, Paul knew, was the most dangerous one in the *kibbutz* — the dugout at the eucalyptus grove.

Jehiel's swarthy face merged with the darkness, but

his eyes glittered as he said, *"Shalom. Hacol beseder."*

"You sound gay," Paul said to Bracha as she clapped her hands to the rhythm of her singing.

"Oh, but I feel good! A state! We'll have a state of our own!" She danced past him, striding into the night with a rifle slung over her shoulder. Brave, good-hearted Bracha, who asked nothing more of God than that there be settlers to cook for, and peace in the Land. Remembering his outburst of a moment before, Paul felt ashamed and humble.

The night air was dry with a stinging sharpness. Mud oozed underfoot, and Paul muttered when he slid and then tumbled into the dugout.

"Ouch! Kindly take your foot off my head!" Ora gave a nervous little titter.

"Sorry!" Paul snapped, shifting away. It would have to be Ora! He groaned inwardly at the prospect of spending the watch with her, even though she seemed in a conciliatory mood.

Ora's nearness made him feel awkwardly self-conscious. It was ridiculous. If he wrote his friends that he was holed up with the most attractive girl in the *kibbutz* and felt uncomfortable about it, there would be no end to their kidding him about it. His hands itched to get at the cigarettes in his pocket, but smoking, he knew, would make an effective target for the enemy.

Pearly clouds floated over the hills, spectral against the dark sky. To the north, the steeper hills could be seen only dimly, as a massed Gothic shadow. The air had the fresh, pungent smell of damp soil, freshly turned.

Paul wondered what to say to break the silence, when Ora volunteered, "A change has come over Erni these past few days. Rina told me. Have you noticed it?"

"It could be he's too frightened to be a nuisance," Paul said.

"It could be," Ora agreed amiably.

They lapsed into silence again. The searchlight, which had been shifting across the fields, swung back abruptly, riveting its long white finger to the wire fence at the eucalyptus grove. It kept probing, as if to ferret out a quarry.

Suddenly, a bullet crashed against the parapet, hurling stones into the dugout. The searchlight swung directly to the hill. Its beam caught and held a cloaked Arab. A spray of bullets hit the ground surrounding him, sending up clumps of earth. The Arab flung out his arm, fingers closed and Ora aimed.

A whistle, a thin mad screech, tore past the dugout. Paul could hear the crackle of thunder as the earth heaved. A flaming cloud took shape in the air, fragmenting itself into orange patches. Smoke puffed upward, swelling.

"The machine shed — petrol's there!" Ora cried, riddling the hill with bullets. The beam of light fastened now to the cleft in the ridge where a moving mass of cloaks cascaded downward.

Gunfire spattered the cleft as the searchlight kept stabbing. The mass of cloaks ceased its downward sweep. To the north, a rosette of lights flickered like distant stars. But the last star had vanished before the settlers climbed out of the dugouts.

Chapter Seventeen

The toll was heavy. Among the dead were Bracha and Jehiel. They were found outside the grove of eucalyptus trees which had been clawed out of the earth.

Noah found them before dawn when he walked the length of the fences, inspecting them, and discovered the gap in the wire. Their bodies, horribly mutilated, lay outside the dugout. With a moan, Noah put his hands to his face to shut out the sight.

Noah's age was his enemy; he no longer possessed the strength necessary for such an ordeal. He stumbled back to the dwellings, unable to rouse himself from his shock, to think through what must be done. He sat on the stone step of the cement building, an old man who had experienced a horror that was now sealed inside him.

An infant broke the dawn quiet with its crying. Noah bestirred himself and hurried to the storehouse where he took some sheets from the shelves. He shrouded the bodies with them.

The sick bay was filled with the wounded. The machine shed and all it contained — the truck, farming equipment, the tractor — were wrecked. Over the *kibbutz* hung the stupified quiet of the stricken.

"Noah, we must have a doctor, medicines..."

"Noah, send for the vet. My Freydele's calf is due."

"Noah, there is no petrol for the cooking..."

He faced the settlers with a hollow calm. "The telephone wires have been cut." They were isolated.

"I will ride to the police post," Ora said.

"With snipers out there!" Dvora cried, seizing her arm.

"Avram is working on the truck. Maybe he will get it to move," Noah said without conviction.

"I'll go," Paul offered. "The police may pay more attention to an American." He avoided Ora's cynical smile. He hadn't meant to flaunt his Americanism, but he knew this to be an advantage.

"Be very careful," Noah cautioned as Paul started out on foot.

Noah waited outside when Sgt. Cassidy went into the storehouse where the coffins were. He saw him stand a moment before Bracha's. Then, doffing his cap, he knelt beside it. He began making the sign of the cross but stopped midway. Noah saw him press his hand to his eyes before he rose.

When Cassidy came out, the scowl on his bulldog face had deepened. "You fools!" he barked. "Is any of this muck worth that girl? If I had my way, I'd arrest the ones that sent the settlers here. Live-bait, that's all you are."

Noah kept silent. He knew his old friend well enough to realize that, for all his ranting, he had no malice for the settlers or the Agency officials, but against the heartlessness of his British officers who confiscated *kibbutz* arms and refused to come to their aid.

They passed the burnt-out machine shed. The acrid smell of smoke still singed the air. Piles of charred timber lay on the ground, while slivers of glass gave off diamondlike glints in the sun. All that remained of the truck was a twist of metal on a dented chassis. Its hood hung awry over the engine.

"It's a miracle the shacks didn't go up in smoke," Cassidy remarked. He glanced at Avram who was dismantling the engine for its usable parts.

"We're entitled to a few miracles," Noah said wryly.

Smiling frostily, Ora walked past them. Cassidy called to her and she turned, but stood where she was with an upthrust chin.

"Why aren't the parapets being rebuilt?" he asked.

"Because we are relying on His Majesty's men to defend us," Ora said in a poisonously sweet tone, and walked away.

"No sense needling him," Avram said, as Ora bent over the engine. "You know where he stands..."

"With the enemy!" she snapped. *"Now* he comes!" Then, waiting until Cassidy was far enough down the road, she said worriedly, "Avram, what if he stays?"

"He won't miss us. After all, he's not here to take another census. Here, I've got more nails." He handed Ora a tin, filled with bent and rusted nails. They were still warm from the fire.

Was it safe, Ora wondered, as she came into the kitchen, to do what must be done, with the police about? But where else? Making bombs was not exactly a kitchen occupation, but the presence of jam tins and powdery stuff was least likely to arouse suspicion here than elsewhere.

The lack of Bracha's quick, efficient presence was evident. The tables and stoves were cluttered with stacks of unwashed dishes, pots and cutlery and the floor was slimy with spilled food.

At the sink, the girls worked listlessly, their faces

blotched with weeping. They nodded unsmilingly to Ora and hurried to clear a table for her.

Ora set to work making the bombs. She rammed the gelignite into the tins, packing them solid, then forced in the nails. She grinned, remembering the shrapnel-like effect of the explosion the last time she had flung them from the rear of the attackers. Then, pressing the fuse down hard into the detonator, she forced both into the tight mixture of gelignite and nails.

Tonight, there would be only Avram and herself making their way to the rear of the attackers on the hill. Avram's brother had not come back from that attack, three months ago. Which of them would return from it tonight?

Even the youngest of the children sensed that today was not a day for singing songs at the piano, and Emmi was hard put to keep them occupied. She was not in a mood for games or stories; she had spent the night tending the wounded. And she was weary with more than fatigue; Bracha was dead.

It was when she was serving lunch in the children's dining room that she saw Alan. As he walked past the children's section, she stepped quickly away from the window but held him in view. He went into the storehouse. He was looking for her! She could not help the fact that her heart hammered with excitement.

By the time the children had finished their meal and attended to the chore of face and hand washing and undressing for their rest period, Emmi's nerves were taut with expectancy. She was due at the sick bay — she had promised to relieve Surele during the children's rest period. But Alan stood leaning against the pickup and she would have to pass him to reach the sick bay. She could not bear to face him.

There was nothing to do but make a detour — turn to the right and go the long way around, in the rear. It was cowardly, she knew, avoiding him.

Instead, she came out — and turned left! It was as if a demon had taken possession of her body and was rushing her toward Alan!

"Emmi! I've been looking for you!"

She tried to speak, but her throat closed on the words.

"I heard about the attacks. I was worried. How are you?"

"Quite well, thank you." Her voice sounded strange to her ears — a high-pitched quaver. She ought to excuse herself and hurry away, but his eyes held hers with a power as if he had gripped her with his arms.

"Emmi, can't we go where we can be alone and talk?"

Until that moment, Emmi had not been aware that Avram was piling stones on the parapet only a short distance away. She flushed darkly when she saw him staring at them.

"What is there to talk about?" she asked, avoiding his eyes.

"About us . . . and all that's happened."

"I'm still alive," she said.

"That job, for instance. I've found people in Haifa, who . . ."

"Will they not mind that I am Jewish?"

"Stop that, Emmi!" he said in sudden anger. "I didn't mean . . ."

"You didn't mean to say it quite that way, but it is what you meant. Your instincts spoke for you. Experience has taught me to know this."

"Emmi, can't we go somewhere to talk? We are being watched."

"Why — are you ashamed of what you did?"

"I'm not ashamed of doing my duty!" His face tightened.

She studied him for a moment as if considering, not the reply, but the man. What had drawn her to him in the first place? It must have been his resemblance to Gunther. He had the same long, narrow face, the brown hair springing off the steep forehead, the same bright blue eyes and, after Shimon's arrest, the same brute hardness in them as Gunther had when he wore the swastika arm band.

"Don't look at me like that, Emmi! I saw the way you looked at me the other day — but a policeman's duty is — like a soldier's. You have no choice — when you're in service. I shouldn't have roughed him up, I know — I only meant to..." He touched her arm and she jerked away from him.

"I don't know what you *meant* to do — I only know what you *did*. And it's something you'll never undo," Emmi said. She turned quickly and walked away.

At the parapet, Avram was forcing small stones into the gaps between the larger ones. He could see Emmi coming and was about to say something sarcastic when the expression on her face silenced him. It was not her usual resigned and lonely look, but something quite different. He could not determine exactly what it meant, but it had something of the expression he saw when she played the piano. It was as if she knew what she was doing, and this made her happy. Without greeting him, Emmi bent down, found some small stones and held them out of him. They worked on the parapet together.

On Sgt. Cassidy's order, the dugout at the eucalyptus grove was not to be manned by the settlers that night. Ora and Avram felt uneasy about this. Did Cassidy plan to occupy the dugout himself? If so, it would be impossible for them to leave the *kibbutz* from that point. They would have to steal away through the gate at which the heaviest fire was always concentrated. Worse yet, after the evening meal, Cassidy kept them all under his vigilant eye.

The sun had barely set when lights began twinkling in the hills. As Ora started down the steps of the cement building, Cassidy called her. Turning, she said airily, "Even your queen must do certain things for herself." Then she walked away.

Returning, a few minutes later, she hoped that Cassidy would not notice how much fuller she was across the chest, or that her jacket was now too tight under the arms. He was giving orders to Alan, and she strained to listen.

"Keep the beam off the *wadi* . . . unless firing is heavy . . . . wait for the rocket from my Verey-light pistol . . . half a pan . . . then have a go at them . . . focus on the cleft of that hill . . ."

Was he, too, planning to surprise the Arabs from the rear? If so, why was he making a mystery of it?

The attack began early. Brief flashes twinkled in the *wadi* near the eucalyptus grove. A crackle of shots broke from the hills and at the cleft of the highest ridge, they could see a flash of white cloaks. Cassidy stood motionless. What was he waiting for? — Ora wanted to scream.

"The firing seems to be coming from the *wadi,* but the concentration is at that cleft in the hill," Avram observed. Cassidy ignored him. Ora clenched her hands. Every nerve in her body was straining to get going.

"Well, let's get on with it," Cassidy said, at last.

"Get on with what?" Ora demanded.

"With what you and Avram planned. Only this time,

you do as I say. Leave off your shoes and put on heavy socks — several pairs of them. And Ora — those white buttons on your jacket — they'll show in the dark. Now get on with you."

"How did he know what we planned to do?" Ora asked Avram as they ran to their tents.

"Noah told him about that first time. He must have guessed we'd make another try for the rear."

When they returned, Cassidy instructed them briefly. They were not to speak, but to whisper, and only if absolutely necessary. And they were to touch each other every few feet, to make certain no one had strayed. Finally, they were to watch the swing of the searchlight — and have patience!

"Only the patient man returns from a mission," Cassidy said.

They started toward the eucalyptus grove. A shell sank into the earth at their feet, sending up a spray of mud. They reached the newly planted vineyard and Ora winced when Cassidy stepped on the plantings.

In the dugout, Cassidy bent down to whisper some additional instructions to Alan. Ora could see, in the dark, the shiny steel nozzle of a machine gun. If they had been allowed to possess such a weapon, Bracha and Jehiel and the others would not be lying in pine boxes, Ora thought bitterly.

They crawled through the torn fence into the fallow field, flattening themselves on the ground when the searchlight swept over them. In its bright glare, Ora could see that Cassidy had blackened his face and torn off his shiny silver buttons. And he had stuck a leafy branch in his cap! He looked so comical that she had to smother a laugh. They waited, listening for a stir of movement or some sound. Then they ran, crouching low, over ground that was wet with yesterday's rain. The mud clung to Ora's feet, forming a bootlike cast over her heavy socks.

The wind rustled through the reeds. Against its murmuring, it was safe to run forward. Then, as the searchlight slashed the dark, Ora pressed herself to the ground. The beam kept gliding over her back and she felt as if her comrades were sending her a message, wishing her a safe return with objective achieved.

The gunfire sounded like the distant crackle of lightning. Pinpoints of lights pricked the darkness in the distant reaches of the *wadi*. Ora began crawling faster. Avram was only a few paces ahead of her, within touching distance.

Again, the searchlight probed, swinging in a quick arc over her head and lighting up the field in a brilliant yellow wash. Ora crouched against the sharp spears of a cactus bush and held her breath, pleading mutely with the beam, *"Chaverim* — move it quickly! Don't make me a target!" The beam swung away.

Her rifle nipped her neck, and her leg had gone numb, but Ora dared not change her position. The beam was probing the ground around her. Now her whole body went numb. Suddenly, the spear of light oscillated, swinging wildly as if it had gone out of control. Then, slowly, it glided back and aimed at a clump of bushes, spraying them with light. Finally, it shifted to the hill.

Ora was in darkness again and she sighed with relief and the luxury of being able to move. The front of her jacket was soaked through with mud. Something scurried lightly across her back. She shuddered, biting a scream into her wrist. Field mice! Ugh! She loathed them.

Again, the lights flickered, gleaming brighter now.

They were coming closer! Her heart thumped wildly. She lay flat, her cheek pressed against the damp earth, and followed with her eyes the movements of the bright twinklings. Suddenly, a light sprang at her hand. It was a tortoise! A tortoise with a small electric torch attached to its back! It wriggled away as she reached out to seize it.

Oh, how diabolically clever they were — my cousins, the Arabs! So, it was at the gleam of these moving lights that they had been firing last night, when all the while the Arabs were shooting from another direction!

Cassidy and Avram must have discovered the ruse, for one by one the lights blinked out. They were crawling uphill now — eastward, toward the ridge. Ora could feel the exposed, bony roots of a tree. The ground was fairly dry here, but the rough bushes scratched her face and hands. She heard the creaking of branches as the wind rushed through them. Something sharp stabbed her neck. It was a twig. Now the thick, inky black of night closed in on her. She reached out to touch Avram.

The sound of firing was closer now. Ora heard the lift of a voice in a drawn-out, ululated cry and she levelled her rifle. Then the hill resounded with Arab yells and she clenched her teeth hard, wanting to fire volley upon volley at those who were screaming *"Itbah lel Yahud!"*

Someone slid against her. Instantly, her finger was on the trigger. Avram's whisper at her ear stopped her.

"They're below us — on the slope — more on the cleft. Climb to the top, count to fifty as you climb. Cassidy needs that much time. Throw the bombs down the slope after his rocket goes off. Keep close to me."

The climb steepened. Vines tangled about Ora's feet and she had to stop to free herself, worrying as she did so that Avram had crawled beyond her touch. She had counted only to thirty when suddenly a brilliant flame lit up the darkness. Cassidy had fired his Verey-light gun!

In its glare, Ora could see Arabs against the farther ridge. The *kibbutz* searchlight began sweeping toward them and a great burst of firing broke out. Ora lit a fuse and hurled a bomb down the slope. Then she flung two more at the ridge. She waited, holding her breath in suspense. She could hear only the rat-a-tat of the firing. Had the bombs fallen into a swamp? Had the wetness of her jacket seeped into the tins?

Suddenly, there was a thunderous roar and huge chunks of earth sprayed upward. In the sweep of the searchlight, Ora saw a frantic scurrying toward the cleft in the hill. Cloaks were flying like unfurled, windwhipped sails. She fired.

Cassidy's gun kept chattering, two shots to every one of hers or Avram's. Oh, if only they had a Lewis gun at the *kibbutz!* Relentlessly the *kibbutz* searchlight speared the fleeing men, illuminating them as targets for the three on the ridge.

Before long, there was no answering fire and, in the glare of the swinging beam, no one stirred on the cleft of the hill. The bareness there, and a sprawl of motionless figures on the slope, brought peace to the night.

The three returned as they had come, crawling through brush and over cold, rain-soaked earth. But victory had warmed their blood and they felt neither the cold nor the dampness, nor even fatigue.

Cassidy wondered if the Arabs would call it quits after tonight or put up another show. This was the first time he had seen them turn tail and run in panic, leaving their dead behind. Twenty men or better would never attack again. The sweep of the searchlight had been too quick for Cassidy to be sure, but it would even a score if it were that many — one dead Arab for each of Bracha's years.

The long yellow beam was like a finger beckoning, guiding them home. Ora wished that Cassidy would let them walk upright. She asked again, but back came the snap of his words, "Get on with it, girl. They might be coming back for their dead, now that it's quiet. Hold your tongue — and no nonsense!" Ora wondered if there would be a need for more pine boxes in the *kibbutz* that night.

Avram was wondering if the look he had seen on Emmi's face that afternoon meant what he had read into it. She had helped him only briefly because she was needed in the sick bay. But each time she had held out a stone to repair the parapet, it was as if she were offering him a gift — something of herself.

At first, he felt only a quick, sharp prick in his leg, engrossed as he was in his thoughts. Soon, however, great burning waves of heat rolled upward from the pain, making him feel as if he were on fire.

There would be no need for pine boxes, as Ora had feared. But there had been casualties. Although the Arabs had been routed, the settlers were in no mood to rejoice. The sick bay was crowded with the wounded — and the mounds in the graveyard were still too fresh with their dead.

Nor was it a consolation to hear, when the radio was repaired that night, that they had fared better than other *kibbutzim*. They had experienced four nights of terror, and the quiet that now lay over Tel Hashava was the morbid quiet of the physically and emotionally spent.

For Emmi, the baptism of fire brought to the surface qualities she did not know she possessed. Neither her days nor her nights knew an idle moment. She looked after the children, helped repair the parapets, tended the wounded and even found time to help Dvora with the cattle. She hurried from one task to another with such urgency that it seemed as if any moment wasted would be fatal to whatever or whoever it was that required her presence.

In the sick bay, she heard her name being called from all sides. Shlomo's bandage had to be changed again. Some shrapnel had to be removed from Dvora's shoulder, from the night's attack, and Emmi held her hands steady with an iron grip while the doctor probed. And Rina's dark eyes expressed tearful gratitude as, later, Emmi sponged her burning body.

It was now long past midnight. Emmi no longer considered the time. It was either dark, and night — or it was light, and day. The doctor had already left when Avram limped in. His strained look and blood-flecked lips, the unnatural glitter in his eyes, alarmed her. Emmi ran out after the doctor.

When she returned with him, Surele had already washed Avram's leg. It was swollen, and a festering wound gaped just below the knee. The exchange of glances between the doctor and nurse frightened Emmi.

"Odd place for a snake bite," the doctor said casually. "Will have to cut it a bit. I'm afraid it will hurt."

"Cut away. Just leave me the other leg to move on," Avram said. His face twisted as a fresh stab of pain went through his leg. Then, forcing a smile, he winked at Emmi. "You look worried. My leg can't be hurting you that much." She returned his smile, wanly.

Avram ground his teeth as the doctor began probing the wound with his scalpel. Emmi held out her hands and he gripped them hard. Sweat began breaking out on his face. When his hands went limp in hers, Emmi knew the doctor had finished.

Almost at once, Avram fell into a deep sleep. Emmi leaned over him and brushed his cheek lightly with her lips. Her mouth felt singed by the heat of his skin. Frantically, she wove around the beds to reach the nurse.

"We are out of quinine and we're out of alcohol to wash him down," Surele said as she felt Avram's forehead.

"Is there any alcohol in eau de Cologne?" Emmi asked. When Surele nodded, Emmi ran out to her tent. The cherished bottle was at the bottom of her trunk and she smiled wryly when she found it. Alan had not intended it for Avram when he gave it to her!

"I smell like an Arab bride," Avram said when he awoke late the next morning as the doctor was examining his leg.

Emmi giggled. The doctor's look had been reassuring — there would be no need to amputate! Learning this, Avram's grin spanned the width of his face.

Dabbing at his fuzzy hair and face with fragrantly moistened cloth while his eyes followed her every move, Emmi wondered why she had never noticed before how expressive Avram's eyes were — and how devilish they looked, when he teased!

"Emmi, your hands are as light as butterflies," he said. Then, with a deep, contented sigh, he fell asleep again.

Nearby, the nurse was waging a losing argument with Dvora, who insisted on getting out of bed. Emmi hurried over.

"My Freydele, she is going to calve tonight, surely — She needs me," Dvora insisted, elbowing the nurse away.

"We can lose the calf — but we cannot lose Dvora!" Emmi said sharply, pressing her back into bed with both hands.

"She is very nervous — she needs to be talked to — petted. Oh, she will lose the calf . . ."

"The others are looking after her. I saw them in the barn," Emmi said. "But if you wish, I will pet Freydele myself, and tell her how worried you are." She smoothed back Dvora's damp, unkempt hair as she spoke. Seizing Emmi's hand, Dvora pressed it to her cheek.

Leaving the barn, Emmi stood a moment, outside, feeling sick about what had happened. She had neither the energy nor the heart to face Dvora with the news — Freydele had died, calving her newborn. She remembered Dvora's anguish the night before, when one of the cows had been felled by a bullet, and she could not bear to bring her fresh pain.

Paul came by as Emmi stood leaning against the barn wall, her small thin figure sagging with fatigue. He saw her put her hands to her face as a sob broke from her, and was deeply moved. Her composure during four murderous night attacks, and the eagerness with which she helped everywhere, had surprised him. But she was feeling a reaction to the ordeal now, he knew. There seemed no hope of a more peaceful and normal existence on the hill land in the future. — He felt profoundly sorry for her.

"Emmi, you ought to be in bed!" he said, touching her shoulder lightly. She gave a violent start.

"Oh, it is all too dreadful!" she sobbed.

Paul took her arm and began walking her toward her tent. "Emmi, if you want to go to America, I think I can help. My parents would make the affidavits for you and Erni . . ."

Shaking her head, Emmi gaped blankly at him. "Oh, but I couldn't! I couldn't leave now! How could I? *They need me!*"

Emmi sounded as though she were rebuking Paul. And she had not even thanked him for his offer of help! With a puzzled frown, as if questioning his good sense, she studied him, shook her head, and then turned and walked briskly back to the sick bay.

There was no end to the miracles that were happening in the Land! Paul thought, smiling.

Chapter Eighteen

The transformation, Emmi thought, had come overnight. Only yesterday, the fields had a dry and withered look and this morning, there was a lovely splash of flowers everywhere — the bright crimson anemone, cyclamen and iris — and the hills were aflame with poppies. Along the slopes of Boulder Hill, yellow-starred daisies and delicate blue lupins could be seen. It was as if the earth had grown weary of its own drabness and had decked itself out in all its floral finery.

Everywhere Emmi looked she saw a waving sea of wheat and barley, while the slips in the vineyard had grown leafy tendrils that spread a soft green cover across the field. Even the cement building was touched with this magic. A spiral of bougainvillea flaunted vivid petals across its face. She felt a pang of regret at leaving all this. The upper hill section to which they were now moving was still harshly bare.

The moving was being done in stages. Three months earlier, the work of clearing and building had begun on upper Tel Hashava and thirty of the settlers had gone to live there permanently, returning every *Shabbat*. For Emmi, this reunion with Avram, Ora and Paul had meant a week-long anticipation of pleasure and friendship.

With the buildings begun on the hill land, the Haifa

members had come to stay in lower Tel Hashava until
the new dwellings were ready for them. Fourteen new
immigrants had joined the *kibbutz,* and a large group
of youths from the Aliyah Youth Training Centre was
due that week. The newcomers would remain here when
the Haifa members finally joined the upper settlement.

It seemed to Emmi that each time she came into the
dining hall, she found herself sitting next to a newcomer.
The previous month, a girl had arrived whose eyes had
the lost look of the uprooted. Remembering her own
unhappiness when she first came, Emmi, who now considered herself a *vattika* — a veteran — befriended her.
She persuaded her to join the Hebrew class, and drew
her into the various social activities. Shlomo soon relieved Emmi of her charge, and only last *Shabbat,* he
and the girl had applied for a room in one of the huts.
This, Emmi knew, was the *kibbutz* way of announcing
a marriage that would later be solemnized by a visit to
a rabbi.

To celebrate the occasion, wine had been added to
the meal. Avram, who always managed to find a seat
next to Emmi, asked in a voice loud enough for all to
hear, "When are we going to drink to our announce-
ment?" Emmi crimsoned at his brashness in proposing
to her in public.

Ora and Paul looked questioningly at Emmi and, em-
barrassed, she lowered her eyes, vowing to teach Avram
a lesson or two about social amenities. She kept picking
at her food as if nothing had happened, but she did not
resist when Avram's hand groped for hers under the
table.

At last, the trucks were loaded. The settlers remaining
in Tel Hashava came out to bid the hill pioneers fare-

well. Dvora, who was leaving two calves behind at whose births she had assisted, was tearfully apprehensive. She kept calling out last-minute instructions to the new barn specialists as the convoy got under way, and promised herself that she would return every *Shabbat* to make sure her "charges" were being properly cared for.

Most of the children who were going sat in the trucks with their parents, but a few insisted on riding with Emmi. These were the younger ones, and Emmi was flattered by their clinging to her.

Erni started tugging at her sleeve. "Will there be Arabs?" he asked.

"Of course!" Emmi replied. Then, seeing worry lines wrinkle his forehead, she added quickly, "But they are friendly Arabs. They exchange visits, and they supplied our water until our own well was dug."

Erni nodded, but seemed doubtful.

"Don't worry," Yigal said. "They know we are good fighters."

"Yes — we are good fighters," Erni agreed, as he held out a string for the game of cat's cradle.

Emmi stared at him, amazed. Erni was speaking *Ivrith!* The wonder of it was not that he *could* — but that he *would!* And he had said, *"We* are good fighters!" How had this transformation come about?

She had been so occupied with her teaching and learning, so engrossed in the pedagogy and child psychology books that Avram had brought her from Haifa, that she had not noticed the change in Erni. Had the attacks frightened him into better conduct, or had he been doing something particularly naughty? *Back there* (and now, Emmi smiled — aware that she had thought, *"back there"* and not *"at home"*) back there, Erni had been most tractable when he had been naughtiest.

Had Yigal replaced her in his affections, she wondered. It was wonderful, of course, that he had a friend, but she could not help feeling a little sad. In gaining this friend, he seemed to have lost his need of her. She put her hand on his shoulder to communicate this sense of loss. He looked up questioningly, then smiled and gave her hand a quick kiss.

Passing through the gate, the lead truck slowed down on the road to wait for the others. Emmi stood up to have a last look around. The conical tents, the wooden huts, the cement buildings, could barely be seen through the luxuriant fields of wheat.

This was the sector she had worked in that first week of her arrival ten months ago. It was a good feeling, seeing the tangible results of her efforts. To the north, Emmi could see the fuzz of green that was the new eucalyptus grove, and the cypress and carob trees she had helped to root after the raiders had torn up the young trees.

With the attacks, she had come closer to the core of life and had related herself more meaningfully, as a settler, to her work. She experienced a wholeness and feeling of contentment that she had not known before. Reflecting on the thoughts that had troubled her, Emmi wondered how she could have let superficial things blind her to what was truly vital and important.

She must never forget that the Land had opened its doors to her when others had shut her out, that she had friends here and — even more important — as Avram had told her many months before, she was where she was *wanted!*

Of course, the *kibbutz* lacked the *gemütlichkeit* she loved, but there was the future to shape — with its more significant objectives. She must never again let small things matter.

Avram came running alongside the line of trucks, waving them forward. The wind caught his hair, tossing it wildly, and the sides of his shirt had pulled loose from his trousers. His manners were crude, Emmi thought, watching him, but basically he was good — and he was brave. But he ought not to be so sloppy!

He paused briefly before her. "Better sit down, Emmi. Too many sharp turns on the road."

She met his eyes with a smile.

Paul noticed the moody look on Ora's face when the truck moved past the little cemetery. There were six markers. And he had known three of those under them. Dov, who had a reverence for all life but his own; Jehiel, the psalm-singer, who had come because of his soul's need to unite himself with ancient roots; and Bracha, the gentle Goliath, who once said, "Just living in the Land puts God's grace on one."

Just past the cemetery lay the last uncleared section in Tel Hashava. Paul could see the new settlers struggling with the stones, heavy ones, that pulled them earthward as they carried them to the wall they were building. He watched them until the truck rounded a curve in the road.

The work was excessively strenuous, and if the same effort were applied abroad, the settlers would surely earn a more comfortable livelihood. Here, they ate frugally and lived crudely — and always in the shadow of violence. They had been toughened by their struggles and yet not made hard by them.

But the future held a hope brighter than any they had known. A state was soon to be declared, and they would be a nation — sovereign, like other nations. Noah had written a song for this new sovereignty and Paul could hear the settlers singing it in the next truck, with Noah's tuneless voice sounding them off key.

Arabs were already pouring across the borders to abort the birth of the new state, but the settlers went on clearing the waste spaces, plowing, seeding, building.

A few days before, when Noah had read a report that sounded like a blueprint for a future Utopia, Paul had asked Ora what was left for the young to accomplish and she had replied, "To attain these goals — and to maintain them." They would survive with their faith intact because their moral strength was equal to their goal, Paul knew.

The American is puzzling over a thought, Ora suspected. He looks as if he is speculating on where all this will lead. He will jot everything down in one of his notebooks and later, the pages will be bound between covers into a book that will be about the Land — and us. But the *essence* escapes him, she thought — as it escapes the others.

The essence is not *survival*. It is *revival*. Rebirth. We want to be what we *were* — the people of the Land. And we don't want to be dead heroes, so that we can become a living nation. Don't praise us with a book, Paul. Praise us with your hands. Stay here and help us build for those who have no other place to go but home — Israel.

Ora sat with her hands clasped around her knees, her luminous dark eyes fixed pensively in space. The sunlight on her face heightened the rosy tints in the copper of her skin. She could hear the thin, high-pitched singing of the children in the truck behind her and the raucous singing of Noah's song up ahead.

For a moment, Ora's thoughts slipped back to what, for months, she had forced from her mind — Hassan. She saw again his anguished look when she had pulled free from his embrace, and she felt wrenched with longing for him. *Hassan, must you hate what you dare not love?* We were friends long before we became lovers. Think back, Hassan, on what you valued in our friendship — and I offer it to you with all my heart. Don't reject it, Hassan, for friendship is love, too, and friendship is peace.

Out of her loneliness, and almost like a healing, there came to Ora a deep sense of her special and peculiar trust. It was not just an accident of birth that had made her an Israeli. Every part of her was linked to her immortal ancestors, who had fertilized this Land with their blood and their bones. Her covenant with them had bound her to the task from which they had been torn. Nothing less — and something infinitely more — they had witnessed an exile — she would serve the redemption. The hill land was not merely a challenge — it was a command — to rise up and build!

The truck began climbing. Upper Tel Hashava, with its small houses and large cement buildings and bell tents, could be glimpsed beyond the giant boulders. They passed the Arab village on the upper hill, its slopes tufted with green and splashed crimson with poppies.

An Arab stood watering his donkey at a ditch. He glanced up as the convoy came by, his dark face screwed up against the brilliant sunlight. Ora waved and listlessly. he waved back.

"My cousin, the Arab," Ora said, smiling at Paul.

Paul thought he detected a hint of irony in her words, but he could not be sure.